I HIRED A HITMAN

ALEXIS ABBOTT

PATHFORGERS PUBLISHING

Get an EXCLUSIVE book, **FREE** just as a thank you for signing up for my newsletter! Plus you'll never miss a new release, cover reveal, or promotion!

http://alexisabbott.com/newsletter

PROLOGUE

*M*y truck tears down the gravel road, spitting rocks up and clinking again the metal. The wind is in my hair, whipping around me. The blue sky spreads out before me, kissing the gold of the land.

I never knew how big the sky could look until I moved to the Midwest. It's strange. Americans think little of the wide-open plains and the rich fields that go on forever, but to me, I can't get enough of it.

It gives me life. This is why I came to this country. This is what brings me peace. This is what freedom looks like.

As the thundering truck engine rumbles under me, I think back to the howling winter winds of Siberia where I was born. And then the high rise towers of the city that blotted out the sky and horizon.

Now, I find myself here in this sleepy farming town. Strange that it took me moving to the other side of the world to find a place that feels like home.

The drive from my modest homestead to town is the same as always. To someone just passing through, it might seem like an endless road with equally endless farmland on either side. I know better, though, and so do the locals.

As the smell of rich earth and seed fills my nose, I pass fields that belong to people who I know just by having driven by them enough times. An older farmer is out on his tractor to the right, while the field on the left is getting worked by a younger man while an older one watches warily. Must be a new hire.

I pass a couple of teenage girls walking down the road outside one of the farms like they always are around this time of day, and I move over on the road out of courtesy to avoid roaring right beside them. The first time I did, the shorter of them got startled, so I make a point to be more conscientious now.

Things are different outside of the city, and I don't want to stand out in the wrong way.

My truck roars into town, but I don't turn many heads. The locals have gotten to know the sound of my truck.

I draw more attention when I bring my motor-cycle through. Even then, the roar of my bike isn't too different from the sound of some of the worn-out old trucks that rumble through on a regular basis, carrying chickens, seed, hay, and anything else that fills the air with that rich country smell.

What I like about this place most is that nobody pays me much mind. I get no questions from them about where I come from, who my connections are, and what I'm doing here.

The very few people I've spoken to know I'm Russian, and they know that I occasionally buy drinks at their bar, keeping to myself in dark corners where I can enjoy the privacy of my own thoughts.

At well over six feet in height, that's all anyone wants to know from me.

I like it that way.

The less they know about my past, the better off we all are.

I pull up to the only real store in town, which I've never visited before today. My chickens need seed, and my horses need hay. I usually buy everything wholesale, but my shipment is late, so I have to make a quick stop to tide the animals over. It's such a pretty day out that I'm itching to be on my bike, but as much as the locals would like to see me try, carrying hay on a motorcycle is something I don't want to test out.

The store is tall and wide, and there are no fancy adornments on it. I'm fairly sure it used to be a warehouse that someone bought and turned into a store. The people around here are hardworking,

ALEXIS ABBOTT

honest, and frugal. They don't bother tearing down
perfectly good buildings to make room for fancy
new ones unless they need to.

The Midwestern US is a bit like Siberia in
that way.

I step into the store, and the woman at the
counter greets me with a gruff smile and a nod of
her head. I return it, and I make my way in.

I loop around the outer aisles to the back of the
store, where I start to make my way toward the seed.
I move quietly, not because I mean to, but out
of habit.

For so many years, moving through buildings
quickly and quietly was part of how I made my
living. I made my body into a walking shadow, a
soundless spirit who could slip through a hotel or a
house or an office with ease. Not a soul could detect
me, if I didn't want them to.

I might have left my old life behind me, but the
skills I honed to perfection are still with me. When
anyone asks why a man my size tends to sneak up on
people, I just tell them I'm a hunter.

It's not far from the truth.

A few aisles before the one where I can find
chicken seed, I pass a young woman who's busying
herself with stocking the shelves.

Her head turns, surprised, and for a fraction of a
second, our eyes meet.

Despite my best efforts, my heart skips a beat.

I notice her by her hair before anything else. It's the kind of very light copper that Americans call strawberry blonde. But as soon as she looks at me, she draws my gaze to her hazel eyes that catch the sunlight and make it dance.

Then, she gives me that smile that melts my heart. Her freckled face and curvy figure draws my eyes. Daisy Jenson. That's the name on the pin just above her left breast. Daisy. *I'd certainly like to pluck her*, I muse, thinking back on the childish games the kids used to play. *Wants me, wants me not. Wants me*, I settle on, my gaze moving forward once more.

That slightest meeting between us scorches me like fire, but the next moment, I move on.

In the past, I might have followed my heart's impulses. I could chat her up at the bar and see where things go—what else is there to do in a small town like this?

I'm here to keep a low profile and live out a quiet life for the time being, not fool around with the locals. I'm a restless man, so I know I might not be able to do that forever, but if I want to try to play the part of a reclusive homesteader, leaving a trail of broken hearts through town isn't the best way to go about it.

But I can't deny that her breathtaking smile and beautiful curves ignited something primal inside of me. I'm smiling as I pass another young man about Daisy's age who doesn't look at me as we cross paths. He's a good-looking guy about my height, which I don't often see, but I figure he's the local heartthrob. Has the look of a sweet country boy about him.

I get to the seed and pick up what I need before heading back the way I came.

Another of the many skills I keep with me from my old life is a sharp sense of hearing.

And when I near the aisle where Daisy is, what I hear makes me freeze.

"Look, we're going out tonight. I already told the guys I'd have you out there, I don't want you makin' me look like a damned fool!"

The low growl of a voice comes from the farm boy I passed a few seconds ago. I'm not in sight of him yet, but I moved so quietly that he must not have noticed me. Slowing down, I take a few steps into the aisle behind where the voice is coming from, and I listen.

His voice sounds angry. I know a threat when I hear one.

"I'm not off my shift until nine tonight, Dean," Daisy whispers back, and I feel my heart rate pick up. She sounds frightened, but she's putting up a fight. "I'm gonna be exhausted." An excuse. A pleasant way to turn someone down when saying something harsher might lead to unwanted consequences. Dean isn't the type of man that takes no for an answer, I can tell that much already.

"Scott said you're off at eight," he snaps. "Don't lie to me, Daisy. I don't like liars."

There's a menacing edge to his voice that makes my fist clench and my jaw set.

"I'm sorry, I meant to say eight," she lies. I can tell she's trying to placate him, her voice dropping into a more soothing tone the way girls are trained to speak to aggressive men. "It's just been a really long day, Dean."

"You told me you'd see me again," he says. "My pa raised me to take people at their word, and I'm gonna do just that."

"I-I want to, I promise," she assures him. "And I'm going to, you just keep asking at bad times."

"I don't care," he says. He sounds like every other young man I've known who has never heard the word 'no' before. "If you keep actin' like this, Daisy, I'm gonna take it personally. When you don't talk to me right, it makes me mad."

"I know, I'm sorry, Dean," she whispers, trying to keep their voices low.

"Not yet you're not," he replies, and I feel my blood boiling. "You keep carryin' on like this, and I'll take matters into my own hands. Understand me, girl?"

My mind is already running through a plan of attack. It's pure instinct. I could drop the seed and slip around the corner, grabbing the man before the bag even hits the ground. He'd be dead before anyone even realized what was happening, and I could be out of the building and speeding away in my truck in less than thirty seconds.

But I take a slow, deep, silent breath and count to ten.

I can't do that.

I can't act on those impulses, even if they're justified.

I am not a hitman anymore.

"I understand," Daisy's thin voice says, barely above a whisper.

Another voice calls from the back of the store, making them both jump.

"Dean? Can I get a hand with the propane back here?"

"Be there in a sec, Scott," Dean calls back, his tone immediately shifted to one of pleasant helpfulness. He's the type of guy that changes on a dime. That's the type of guy that's *truly* dangerous. There's enough of a pause for me to know that he's giving Daisy one final look. I can picture it so perfectly in my mind's eye that it's painful.

I don't want to let this happen to her.

But I can't break away from my priorities, or it could cause more trouble for this tiny town than even Dean must cause.

By the time Dean appears from the aisle and starts heading to the back of the store, I'm already halfway to the register, where I set the chicken seed down. Out of the corner of my eye, I notice Daisy making her way to the employee bathroom in the kind of gait of someone in a hurry who's trying not to let anyone know she's in a hurry.

"Three bales of hay, too," I add, and the woman at the register gives me a nod and a smile.

"You own this place, don't you?" I ask.

The woman looks surprised to have heard me speak, much less ask her a question. After a beat, she puts on another one of those customer service smiles.

"Head manager, but I might as well own it," she chuckles.

"It is a nice place," I say, and it's only when I'm talking with a local that I realize just how much my light accent stands out. "Your employees are mostly the local kids, yes?"

"Well, hard to call 'em boys anymore," she says with a chuckle. "Most of 'em are in their early twenties now. Daisy's the only gal I have here—don't expect her to be here too long, though, that one's got a restless heart. But sure, Dean, Scott, Andy—they're all from around here." She raises an eyebrow, looking a little concerned. "Why? One of 'em didn't give you no trouble, did he?"

The fact that she had to ask makes me curious.

"No," I say simply. "I live outside town, and I've been thinking about paying one of them to tend my chickens if I have to go out of town in the next few weeks." It's a lie I come up with on the spot. I've had to come up with enough such lies on the fly that I can deliver them with a straight face, even to law enforcement.

"Ah, I gotcha," she says, glancing around the store briefly. "If it were me, I'd just ask one of the neighbors to do it."

I nod without a word, but a curious look, and the woman scratches the back of her neck.

"Not to make you think they're not good workers," she adds, chuckling. "They can just get a little rowdy sometimes. Boys will be boys, you know."

There's another one of those strange American phrases, *boys will be boys*. It is not one I appreciate as much, even though I know the meaning much better.

"I see," I say. "Thank you."

"Come to think of it, don't think I've seen you in here before, and I don't think we ever properly met," she says suddenly, changing the subject with a smile. "Name's Jolene." She extends a rugged hand for me to shake, which I accept. After a firm pump, I introduce myself.

"Alexei."

"Ahh, so you *are* Russian," she says with a grin.

That makes me chuckle.

"Hay's on the house, first time customer," she says. "Call it a belated welcoming gift."

"I appreciate it, Jolene," I say simply. I got the

information I came for, and I don't want to dawdle too long. "Take care."

I head out of the store and walk around to the side of the building to the stacks of hay. But as I examine the bales, I hear the sound of Dean's voice from around the corner. I catch the tail-end of his words, but he sounds like he's talking about livestock.

". . . and let me tell you, I've never been gladder to put down a cow like that," he says to the sound of a couple other guys chuckling. "The fat old cow nearly kicked me enough times that she had it coming. I took my time with her, made sure she felt it. They say it makes the meat bad, but I ain't never heard anyone complain."

My mouth twists into a grimace as I realize what the young man is talking about.

He threatens women and likes to torture animals?

I pick up the hay bales while the men behind the store launch into more stories about troublesome slaughters they've carried out around the ranch, and I feel my stomach twisting up. I've only heard two conversations from this Dean, and both of them stir up an angry fire in my heart.

The world would be a better place without such cruel men.

But I remind myself what I need to do to keep a low profile.

Swallowing my impulses, I carry the hay and load

it into the back of the truck with the seed. I climb in and start the engine, pulling out of the lot and tearing back down the same road I always use.

But I know myself too well.

This isn't the last time I'm going to cross paths with these men.

Especially if they're giving a young woman in town trouble.

DAISY

I sit up in bed with a gasp, my hazel eyes wide and fearful. At first, I think that thunderous calamity must be bad weather. A freak storm like the ones we do sometimes get out here on the prairies. Those dark clouds just roll in out of nowhere and light up the sky like the Fourth of July, hammering down on the roof and making the world feel like a ship tossed on the sea.

But I realize slowly that the night sky is calm, the wind barely ruffling through the maple trees outside my window. It's not nature beating at my door. It's man. And I already know by instinct exactly which man it is.

My heart is thumping so loudly I worry that he might hear it. I know he can smell my fear. He can sense the adrenaline pumping through my veins. He can feel the goosebumps on my skin, the sweat rolling cold and shivery down my spine.

He can tell how frightened I am, how strongly his presence can affect me without his even having to try very hard. Sometimes I think that's why he's so interested in me in the first place. It isn't enough for some predators to just kill their prey— they aren't satisfied unless they get to play with it first.

And to Dean Ashcroft, I'm nothing but a helpless prey animal.

It feels almost as if the whole house is trembling, the bare bones of the decades-old foundation shaking with every pound of his fist against the front door.

He's followed me home again, but not like a sweet puppy trailing after a little girl to her house. Like a killer stalking his victim, intruding into her world to remind her that there is no true escape, no real safe place to hide from him. If he wants to find me, he will.

My bedroom is all the way across the house, at the back of the building. And yet, I can feel the vibrations through the whole place. I swear I can almost smell the foul taint of booze on his hot breath.

He's not the man everyone thinks he is.

Dean knows how to hide his true self from the world. He wears a mask, a mighty fine one, well-made and convincing to those who only know him at a surface level. If you went into the local diner or stopped into the hardware shop to ask a local what they might think about Dean Ashcroft, they'd smile and tell you he's a good ole boy. A farm boy. A good kid with a sensible head on his shoulders.

"Now, that's a man who knows how to respect his elders and treat a lady right," they might tell you with a smile. *"Dean is an upstanding citizen and a good-lookin' son of gun, to boot. Any young lady would be lucky to be the belle on his arm."*

Hell, I believed the hype myself when I first met him. He seemed so polite, so well-raised and affable. The kind of guy who smiles a lot and says "please," "thank you," and "ma'am." But it's all for show.

I'm learning that now.

"Open up, Miss Daisy! I know you're in there!" he shouts, his voice only slightly muffled by the thick oak door.

I swallow hard and glance around the room, wishing I kept my shotgun closer by. It's in the closet on the other side of the room, and normally that's a little too close for comfort as is. I have never been a big fan of guns, even though I have grown up around them all my life out here in the country.

Besides, that shotgun is just for show. It's an antique, a vintage piece of machinery bequeathed to me when my father passed away of cancer a couple years ago. It's one impressive-looking item, and I keep it shiny and gleaming like my father always did

— just one of the ways I try to maintain his legacy here at the farm— but it's mostly useless, especially in my hands.

I don't even own the shells for it. I just keep it around as a tool to make myself look more intimidating on the rare chance I might get an intruder or something. Not that I ever have.

So I've never had much of a need for a real gun with real bullets. Until now. Until Dean Ashcroft happened. I have been such a fool to even let him get close to me in the first place...

"Daisy Jensen!" he yells more viciously. His voice cracks and I can nearly hear the alcohol in his tone. "Open this goddamn door before I take it off its hinges!"

I whimper at the sound of his voice, pulling the sheets up to my neck and cowering in bed. I'm terrified to even move or breathe too hard. Not that it matters. He already knows I'm here. My clunky old blue truck parked off to the side of the house makes that abundantly clear. I silently swear to myself, wishing I didn't have such a gigantic, obvious vehicle to make my presence known. If only I had some little moped I could tuck away in the shed...

"I will burn this old shack to the ground! Don't you test me, princess!" Dean shouts, with cruel amusement. "I'm not here to play games, but I will if you make me. And trust me, sweetheart, when I play, I always win!" He pounds on the door several more times, with such intensity that I can see dust motes being shaken down from the ceiling to land on my bed.

I can't take it anymore. I throw the sheets off of myself and swing my legs over the edge of the bed, my heart racing as I hurry to get dressed. On these balmy summer nights I usually just sleep in a thin slip and panties—one of the few benefits to living alone. But tonight, I'm regretting that choice.

On tiptoe and barely allowing myself to breathe too heavily, I rush across the room and quietly open up my armoire. My hands are shaking as I rifle through the drawers, looking for something more substantial to put on. I don't know yet where the hell I'm planning to go, but I know I have to get out of here, whatever it takes.

I whip out an old floral sundress I got at a church yard sale years ago and tug it on over my head, not even bothering to take off my slip dress first. Then I pull on a white knitted cardigan and slide my feet into a pair of soft ballet flats, foregoing my usual boots for something quieter.

I need to be quiet, unobtrusive.

And yet, I also need to move quickly.

It hits me once again how much like a prey animal I have become as a result of knowing a man like Dean. I am no longer the tough, proud, self-assured country girl who runs her own household and takes care of herself.

He has reduced me to something softer and quieter, someone so fearful and nervous I can hardly recognize her face in the mirror these days. That's the part that makes me so upset, to be perfectly honest. I miss feeling so sure of myself. I miss having nothing in this world I feared. Dean Ashcroft has taken that sense of freedom away from me, and that is the sorriest thing he's ever done to someone, I bet.

I open up my closet door, wincing at how loudly it creaks and whines in its rusting hinges, and I gingerly reach to take out that old shotgun. It's heavy and unwieldy in my untrained hands, and I hold it at arm's length as though it's a bomb that might go off at any second. I hastily remind myself that it doesn't have a bullet in it and hasn't been cocked in probably at least a couple decades, and I hold it closer to my chest with some hesitation. Even though it's useless as a weapon, I am hoping that it just might give me a few more seconds of bluffing time if the situation comes right down to it.

But lord, do I hope it doesn't go that way.

I know there's no point in trying to talk to Dean. That's what he wants. To intimidate me into opening that front door and letting him inside. Just like he knock-knock-knocked on my heart and asked to come into my little universe.

Except back then he was more polite, even if that dark intention was secretly there all along. I knew I should not have fallen for it. I should have kept that boy at a distance and let him fantasize about me from afar. But he's like a damn vampire. Once you break down and give him that invitation to come in, he'll just about drain every drop of life out of you without a second thought. I bet if a detective was to dig up Dean's past, he'd find a long, lonely trail of girls drained of vivacity and turned into empty shells.

Luckily, I still have at least a few more drops of life left in me, and I intend to fight for them with every ounce of strength and determination I got. He can't take everything away from me, not without one hell of a fight, and my daddy didn't raise a coward.

I tiptoe over to the wide bay window at the side of my bedroom. Tonight there's a full moon hanging in the sky, like a luminous face winking down at me. There's this old country song my dad used to play all the time about the moon keeping score between the sinners and the saints.

I would like to think that tonight, she's looking after me. Rooting for me. At the very least, the moon will help to guide my way as I sneak out the window and make a run for it. I only hope my legs don't let me down.

"Daisy! Don't make me come in there! We can do this the easy way or the hard way, and I have a feelin' you're not gonna like it the hard way," he snarls, whacking the door with his fists several more times. I take the opportunity while he's making such a racket to unlock the window and slide the pane up to open it.

His knocking drowns out the sound of the latches, thankfully.

A gust of warm midnight breeze ruffles my strawberry-blonde hair. I bite my lip, peering out the window nervously. No. This won't work. The bedroom is still too close to Dean. He will see me climbing out and catch me like a butterfly in a net. And if I even think about heading to the other end of the house, he will see me. The front door has a big pane of crystal in the center of it which will give him a clear view of the staircase. If I go downstairs, he'll see me instantly.

Another idea occurs to me. Not even bothering to close the window, I clutch the gun to my chest and tiptoe out of the bedroom, to the next room over. It's an old-timey bathroom complete with a claw foot tub, and there's a small, square window higher up by the ceiling. I wonder if I can even fit through there. When I was a rebellious teenager, I sneaked out of there a few times. Not to do anything too risky or anything. Usually I just met up with my girlfriends to have a little bonfire out in the woods. No underage smoking or drinking involved.

I could almost smile at the memory if I wasn't so terrified right now. I used to think I was so tough.

I need to channel that rebellious spirit right now.

I hurry across the bathroom and climb up to

stand on the toilet, looking down at my presumed escape route. I will have to shimmy through the window, drop down onto the stooping roof, and drop down. From there, I will bolt to my truck on the side of the house. I keep the keys in the front seat, just like everybody else who lives out here.

With the exception of Dean Ashcroft, there's not a soul in this town that would even think about messing with someone else's property. There's a sort of innocence and trust here in this town, but the likes of Dean might just be enough to scrub that naiveté right out of my heart.

I realize with a jolt of dismay that I can't carry that antique gun and climb through the window at the same time, so I set the gun down on the sink counter and turn back to the window. I hold my breath, waiting for the right moment.

One, two, three… and the pounding at the front door starts up again.

While the house is shaking with that racket, I quickly slide the window open and hoist myself up. Even with my hands shaking, I have to be strong. And fast. It's a tight squeeze, as my curves have filled out quite a bit since I was a teenager, but I manage to scrape my way through. With the night air blowing through my hair and lifting up the hem of my sundress, I carefully scoot down the roof, trying not to lose my footing. When I get to the edge, it seems farther down than I remembered. I know that landing is going to hurt. But it's too late to turn back now.

I jump down, letting out an involuntary gasp at the sharp jolt of pain radiating up through my calves. I nearly crumple to the ground, but I know I don't have time to wait for the pain to pass. I have to run, even if it hurts like hell.

Especially because now that the banging has stopped, I can hear a much more horrifying sound: footsteps. Coming my way. He must have heard my gasp. I pick myself up and start running, my heart pounding so fast I can hardly breathe. I have never been so afraid in my life.

"Daisy, you little bitch!" Dean screeches. His voice is closer behind me now, and I dare not even glance back. I round the corner of the house so quickly that I almost fall, my legs feeling like jello.

My dad's trusty old truck sits dewy and peaceful in the evening mist, and I use every last fiber of strength in my body to make a dash for it. With Dean's boots thumping only a few yards behind me, I fling open the door to the truck and leap into the front seat. I fumble for the keys in the dim light, muttering nonsensically to myself.

"Come on, come on, oh god," I whisper frantically. Finally my fingers close around the keyring and I jam the key into the ignition, almost snapping the thing in half as the engine roars to life after a few stutters. The high beams flicker on instantly and I glance up to see Dean Ashcroft, in his flannel and cowboy boots, illuminated in the eerie glow. There's a wild look in his brown eyes, like a rabid coyote with his teeth bared.

"Shit!" I yelp, jerking the wheel to the right and plowing through the tall grass as I peel out toward the gravel road.

"You little—" he screams. I glance up at my rearview mirror to see him dashing for his own truck to chase me. My chest is heaving with panicked breaths as I switch off my headlights and trundle off into the dark wooded path. There's only one gravel road that leads into town, but what Dean probably doesn't know is that there is a dirt path that takes a longer way 'round. It's a narrow, harrowing trek through the thick trees, especially in a big ole clunker like my truck, but I've grown up in these woods. I know the way. I know every twist and turn, every downed tree and rocky outcropping. I can follow the whispering creek all the way to the outskirts of town even without the lights on to guide me. Tonight, the moon will have to be enough.

After a while, I can't even hear the rumble of Dean's truck on gravel. I'm far enough out of the way that I must have lost him. But I know it's not safe for me to return home right now. And besides, I'm too keyed up. I don't want to be alone. I need to be somewhere public. Somewhere with other people. But it's the middle of the night in a small town where everything closes after supper time. Except for one place.

The Sugar Creek Tavern. That little farmers' bar on the edge of town.

I take a deep breath and make that my destination. After about a half hour of rumbling through the woods, I come rolling out under a streetlight and pull onto the lonely highway, the only street in town to boast the need for an intersection light.

From there it's only a few more minutes until I pull into the little gravel parking lot behind the bar. I put the car in park, turn off the trembling engine, and breathe slowly. I lean forward and close my eyes for a moment, just resting my forehead on the steering wheel while I gather my wits.

I made it.

At least for now, I should be safe. Who knows what fresh hell tomorrow may bring, but tonight, I'm okay.

I slide out of the truck and realize with a sigh of relief that my wallet is under the front seat, where I usually keep it. I have a feeling that's another strange country custom nowhere else in the world is familiar with, but right now I'm mighty grateful. This time, though, I lock up my truck and take my wallet and keys in with me as I walk through the crooked door of the bar, under the flickering green neon sign.

As soon as I walk in, I'm overwhelmed by the

smell of whiskey and tobacco, mingled with the scent of cedar. The bar is small, hardly larger than a trailer, with wood paneling and deer antlers mounted on the walls. An ancient jukebox in the corner is mournfully churning out sad old country tunes, the likes of which my father used to sing.

There aren't a lot of customers in here tonight, and the clientele who are up this time of night aren't the liveliest folks. There are a couple of silent old men with tall hats and thick white mustaches playing billiards in the back, and a few more men seated several stools apart at the bar counter. I stroll up to the counter and take a seat, trying not to draw much attention to myself.

The bartender turns and does a double take when he catches sight of me, and confusion clouds his expression for a second before he remembers he's supposed to play it cool. He walks over and asks in a low voice, "Miss Daisy, I know it's been a few years since I saw you last, but are you really old enough to be drinkin' yet?"

I smile warmly, his familiar face dawning on me. He used to be a regular customer of my father's at the mechanic shop he ran up until his passing.

"Mr. Redd," I greet him. "It's been a longer time than you remember, I think."

I pull out my ID and hand it to him. He smiles, shaking his head and clucking his tongue. He looks back at me and lays my card down on the counter.

ALEXIS ABBOTT

"My, my. Time does go by so fast these days, doesn't it, sweetheart?"

I nod.

"Yes, sir. It sure does."

"What're you havin' tonight?" he asks, leaning on the counter.

I bite my lip, realizing that I have no clue what it is I want. These days I don't have much time or cash to go drinking. I default to the order my dad used to always repeat: "Whiskey on the rocks, please, Mister."

A look of wistful sadness crosses his face and I know he's thinking about my Daddy. But he taps the counter and says, "Yes, ma'am. Comin' right up."

As he's bringing it back to me, I reach for my wallet to hand him some cash, but a tall, broad-shouldered stranger in a leather jacket sidles up next to me and says in a low, raspy voice, "That'll be on my tab, Redd. Along with whatever else the lady likes."

ALEXEI

*D*aisy looks up at me in surprise and confusion, as if she's looking at a stranger. The next second, a flicker of recognition comes over her face, and she bats her eyelashes at me.

"Oh, I remember you. You were at the store today," she says, and she brushes a lock of her hair behind her ear. "Sorry, I'm a little jumpy tonight. What was that for?"

She says it with a friendly smile on her face even though I can tell she's a little shaken about something. I don't have to wonder what that something is, after what I saw at the store.

"You seem like you could use a drink," I say with a reassuring smile.

"That's an understatement," she says with a soft laugh of her own. Her laugh suits her beautifully.

Still, there's a hint of suspicion in there that doesn't surprise me. She's wary of strangers buying her drinks, as she should be.

I'm not going to push her far here, if she doesn't want it. But the moment I saw her come into the bar, I knew I couldn't just let her come and go. She's been on my mind all day. Her beauty. Her troubles.

This is a woman who needs help. The least I can do is find out a little more.

Our drinks arrive, and she quickly takes a sip of hers while I do the same. She clearly needs the alcohol and wants a mouth full of something that doesn't make introductions any more awkward than they inevitably will be.

"I don't think we've actually met," I say.

"You're not in the store too much, if we haven't met," she quips.

"This is true," I admit. "I'm not in town as much as I would like. It's a nice place."

Her face shows a little confusion as she listens to me speak a longer sentence, and her eyes widen in understanding as she registers my accent.

"Oh! Oh. I knew you weren't from around here, everyone knows everyone. But I didn't realize you were from…" She trails off, wincing as she realizes she doesn't exactly know where to guess I'm from.

"You can say Russia," I assure her with a smile, "you'd be correct."

She laughs, relaxing a little.

"Sorry, there's not really a way to ask that without it being awkward. And I guess calling attention to that doesn't help, huh?" Her face gets shades of pinker as she talks, and I can't keep a smile off my face. Finally, she nervously runs a few fingers through her hair and extends a hand. "Hi, I'm Daisy, and I don't know how to stop talking."

"Alexei," I say, taking her soft hand in mine and giving it a gentle shake. "Daisy is a nice name."

"I could say the same of yours," she says, eyes sparkling. "You don't exactly get many Alexeis around here."

"No," I say, "I can tell."

"Nobody's given you any trouble about that, have they?" she adds, looking a little concerned.

I raise my eyebrows and look up and down at my tall, broad-shouldered physique, denim pants, and leather jacket ensemble.

"If they do, it's behind my back and far away from me."

She giggles, and by now she's twirling a lock of hair around her finger. I can't help but stare at that finger, her hair catching the dim light and seeming to almost sparkle as she plays with it. She's enchanting.

"So," I say, the smile fading from my face, "it sounds like you've had a rough day."

"What makes you think that?" she asks, tilting her head to the side. She's testing me.

"You came in looking like you've seen a ghost," I say, listing things off. "And unless you and the bartender have a running inside joke, this is your first time drinking here. *And* you accepted a drink from a big Russian stranger," I finish with a smile. "That hints at a rough day if I've ever had one."

Those long lashes flutter again, and she seems more than a little surprised at my observations.

"Don't suppose you're a detective, are you?"

"No," I laugh, more heartily than I should have.

If she only knew the truth of how wrong she was...

"Well yeah, it may be a small town, but we have our stressful days too. I uh..." She pauses for a moment, and in that second, I know she's about to lie to me. "You know, just a perfect storm of stuff. Couldn't sleep last night, late for work, some road trippers passing through town making life hard, that kind of thing. It's always the little stuff that adds up and boils over, you know?"

"Sure," I say casually. "Those little things can eat away at you, though, if you have to work with them every day."

She pauses for a moment, and I can see the gears of her mind turning, wondering what I'm getting at. She dismisses it the next moment, putting on a smile.

"Of course, right, yeah. So, you live outside town, or...?"

I nod and jerk a thumb westward. "I have what I suppose you would call a homestead a few miles west of here. Just a quiet little place I have to myself, and I have almost everything I need there. There isn't really anything out there to come bother me—nobody demanding my attention, you know?" I add pointedly, raising an eyebrow at her.

She knocks back another gulp of her drink, and I suspect she's catching on to what I'm hinting at.

"Sounds nice," she admits. "Do you work around here or something? One of the farms?"

"No," I say. "I worked hard to build up some savings," I say, and it's only a lie of omission. "I'm out here living off that and taking some time to work with my hands on a house I can be proud of. Call it soul-searching."

It's either an understatement or a downright lie. You don't live with the things I've done and want to spend too much time looking inwards. At least, no one else I know from the life ever wanted to reflect on any of it.

She looks at me, skeptical, but she doesn't call me out on it. I wonder if she's always had good instincts for a lie, or if it's a skill she's had to adopt more recently.

"And how's that treating you?"

"It beats having the kind of day job where you can get cornered by the wrong kind of people," I say, and I look her straight in the eye, my gaze full of purpose.

She bites her lip and closes her eyes a moment. She knows I overheard what happened with Dean. I can see her thinking. She can still back out if she wants to, and I'm truly curious whether she will. All it would take is to ask me to give her some room, and she wouldn't have to answer any uncomfortable questions.

"How much of that did you hear?" she finally asks, lowering her voice to nearly a whisper.

"Enough to know the man who was cornering you is a special and dangerous kind of man," I say, lowering my voice as well. I take a long drink of my whiskey and set the glass down. "I know that tone when I hear it in a man, Daisy. What happened between you two?"

She frowns and hesitates another moment.

"You don't have to tell me," I admit, "but it might be in the interest of your safety."

"No, you're right," she breathes, rubbing her forehead and taking a swing of her drink. "Just...don't go talking about it to everyone in town, will you?"

"Do I look like the kind of person who tells anything to everyone in town?" I asked.

"Yeah alright, fair enough," she says. "That guy you heard, Dean. He works with me, and we've known each other a long time. Everyone has, around here. I... I let him take me out on a date once, not too long ago. Finally caved to him."

"Did he do something to you that you didn't want?" I asked, my tone growing more serious.

"No," she said quickly. "Well, not at first. He wouldn't leave me alone after that first time. At all. He'd corner me at work like that and tell me to go out again, and he hasn't been taking no for an answer. You saw what he's like. And—god, why am I telling a stranger all this?" She runs her fingers through her hair, but I gesture for the bartender to bring us another round.

"Because it sounds like it didn't stop there, and you're afraid it's going to get worse," I say as the bartender sets our drinks before us. "You need someone to tell, as much as you need that drink. Someone who won't judge, and someone who doesn't think he's a... *good old boy*," I say, hoping I got the phrasing right.

"Can't say I'd argue with that," she says ruefully, finishing off her first drink. "Yeah, something happened. He showed up tonight. At my house."

I leaned forward, furrowing my eyebrows. She went on.

"I... I don't know what he was planning. I never thought it would come to this. He seemed really prim and put together when we first started talking, but..." She shakes her head, a frightened look on her face. "He showed up outside my place shouting to high heaven, trying to get me to come down to him. He's gotten bolder and bolder the more I keep turning him down. I tried to sneak out to the truck, but he heard me and almost caught me. He... god, the way he looked when I got to the truck and turned the headlights on him."

Her guard down, I can see more of her shaking, frightened eyes, and it fills me with anger and compassion for her.

I put a hand on her bare shoulder, feeling that soft, peaches and cream skin under my rough hand. She feels so sweet, and she looks up at me with a twinkle of something in her eyes. I open my mouth to speak.

Instead, the door swings open, and in strides a group of no less than seven young men I recognize in passing from around town. One of them gives a long, loud cheer as the first one of them to come in orders a round of bourbons for him and his friends.

"...and keep 'em comin'," he says, "because my boy Troy here just got engaged, and we're gonna tear it up 'till close!"

A moment later, someone finds the jukebox and replaces the sad, slow music with one of the Top 40 pop country songs. When the guys got to dancing and shouting and finding dance partners throughout the bar, the cozy, sleepy venue becomes a madhouse.

Daisy looks jarred, eyes scanning over the group of guys in a near panic.

"He's not with them," I assure her, my fingers lightly cupping her jaw and guiding her gaze back to me. Her shoulders are still as tense as they were when the rowdy boys made their entrance.

She needs a calmer night than what they're here for.

"Sorry," she says, suddenly looking embarrassed. "I'm just jumpy."

"You have a right to be, but don't worry, I'll keep an eye out with you," I say. I nod to a far corner of the bar, a ways away from the rest of the crowd. "In the meantime, want to dance?"

"Hell of a time to dance," she says with a weak grin.

"As good a time as any," I say, standing up and returning it as I take her hand and lead her toward the back. "Besides, a distraction will be good for you."

"So what do they know about dancing in Russia?"

"I don't think we want to start the night off with Russian dancing," I say, barely holding back a hearty laugh. "Maybe for a different crowd that's had a lot more to drink. I've lived here long enough to know what you're all about out here."

We get to a somewhat more secluded corner, as secluded as we could hope for with the new crowd bustling in, and I don't wait to take her hand and start leading her in a dance.

I don't start off slow. That has never been my

style when it comes to dancing, and the music doesn't call for it tonight. Her hand feels soft and warm in mine, and I can feel her heartbeat getting faster through it as I twirl her around and get started.

I didn't realize how much of a distraction she needed until we started picking up speed. Her eyes only leave me every now and then to look to the door, and when she's turned away from me, I do the same. I've learned how to be subtle about where my gaze travels.

I want to keep her safe, but watching her as much as possible makes her *feel* safe.

"You're good," she says after a few minutes of our bodies moving in tempo with one another, and I watch her smile grow with every passing minute. "You do much dancing back home?"

"I haven't been home in a long time," I say. "I like American dancing more."

"That'll make you some friends around here real quick," she says as she brushes up against me, and I let my hand slide over her soft hips as we dance closer.

"I like the one I've made so far," I say, and she goes pink in the face, but she hides it by turning it away from me with a bashful smile.

"You see a lot of the same faces around here after a while," she says. "It's nice to meet a new one... and a new one who knows what he's doing, to boot," she adds.

I pull her up against me at the end of the song, one arm on her hips and the other holding her hand. "You don't work your way across the world without knowing what you're doing."

As the night wears on, we alternate between dancing and taking breaks to get an icy drink to cool us off. Of course, the alcohol doesn't help with that in the long run, but it helps loosen up Daisy. And the more she loosens up, the more I realize she just how much she needs it.

A new kind of song starts up, this one a little dirtier than the last few. I notice that most of the guys around the bar have a girl wrapped around them by now, some of them sitting and lost in each other's embrace, others still up and dancing.

I look to Daisy with a questioning smile, nodding to the dance floor with a raised eyebrow.

"You wanna go there with me?" she asks, her voice tinged with just enough alcohol to have her speaking her thoughts more loosely than usual. There's a playful smile with her words as she stands up. "I sure wouldn't stop you."

"That's what I like to hear," I say, and I get her back out on the dance floor. "Not many women would want to be dancing with a stranger after the kind of night you've had."

"Are you kidding?" she laughs as I spin her around and press my hips up against her rear, my cock swelling at the feeling of her round ass pressing into me. "After the night I've had, you're *exactly* what I need."

I grind against her, and she pushes herself against me as we dance more slowly, sensuously, but by no means classy. These are country folk, and they're all here to have a good time with no pretense.

I can appreciate that.

My hands move up and down her sides, and when I squeeze her hips, she responds by getting closer to me, always moving into my grasp, never away. The way our bodies move, there's no confusion, no missteps, even though we've only just met.

We get lost in the sensation, and every time our eyes meet, it's like those half-seconds in the store drawn out for an eternity.

She turns around and drapes her arms over my shoulders, smiling at me meaningfully. I've been with many women before, but something about the way Daisy looks at me electrifies my whole body in a way I can't explain.

"I don't wanna go home, Alexei," she says, and there's a tinge of sadness to her voice. I realize she's been waiting to say this, and it's only now coming out. "I don't know what's gonna happen when I do."

"You don't have to," I reply in a low husk. "I have room at my place. Nobody would bother you there."

"I was hoping you'd say that," she says with a soft smile, looking relieved.

"Let's get out of here," I say. She nods, and I lead her toward the back entrance.

I hold the door open for her, and as she heads out, I look behind her at the dancers and the front door.

And stepping in through the front door at the very same second is Dean.

I see his beady eyes scan the bar, and just before Daisy disappears into the darkness outside, his gaze falls on her, and his eyes go wide. The next second, those cruel eyes lock with mine.

I give him the iciest glare I've ever given. It's silent, and I make no movement with my hands, but he knows damn well it's a warning to stay back.

Before he can even react, I turn my back on him and walk out, hurrying Daisy toward my truck. She doesn't need to know what just happened.

DAISY

My heart is pounding so fast it feels like a little sparrow trapped in a cage, fighting to burst free and fly away. It's taking all of my strength just to keep my head on straight, to keep from gasping at how wild a turn this night has taken.

It's almost difficult for me to believe that I started out this evening in my bed, listening fearfully as Dean Ashcroft slammed his fist against my front door. I glance at the glowing green numbers on the truck stereo. The time reads 2:13 AM.

I can't honestly remember the last time I was even awake at two in the morning, much less out and about. I work hard at my job, taking on the longest shifts my manager will allow me to have. I have spent so much time playing catch up, trying to keep my life afloat in the years following my daddy's death. I was only eighteen when I lost him, and even though he did his best to teach me how to be resilient and resourceful, both of us thought we would have a lot more time together for him to teach me more.

Of course, fate doesn't give a damn about your plans, and so I lost him way too soon. Way too early. And ever since then I have been scrambling, constantly scrabbling together cash from wherever I could seize it. Hell, I haven't bought a new pair of shoes or a jacket in at least a year. I live a frugal, quiet life, and apart from the folks I talk to at work, it's a pretty lonely existence, too.

And I most certainly have not been spending any time around good-looking, mysterious, powerful men in bars.

I can't even remember the last time I made it out to one of those semi-annual barn dances this little town is so fond of throwing. In high school, that was the thing to do. My friends and I would get all gussied up, put on our flounciest skirts, and angle for a cute boy to ask us to dance. I guess in comparison to what they do at nightclubs in the city, our little country dances were pretty tame. One might even call them lame. But I always had fun, dancing with my friends and talking and laughing way into the night.

Nowadays, though, almost all of my old friends have shipped off across the country for university, leaving me behind along with all those dusty old memories. When Daddy first got sick, I put off my big-time college dreams to stay back here in my hometown and help out at the mechanic's garage alongside him. Everyone probably thinks it was some huge, horrible sacrifice on my part, but the truth is, I made that decision without a moment's hesitation. My dad needed me, and I was not about to abandon him.

Of course, now I'm having to sell off the garage. I can't run it like Daddy used to, and there's no use in it going to waste. Hopefully someone'll come along and my Dad's legacy will live on in that store.

Straight out of high school, no prospects in mind, and suddenly orphaned. It took me some time to pull myself together and find work at the Farm 'n' Feed.

Luckily, this is a small town, and we all know each other. If one of us gets into a pinch and needs some money, all we have to do is ask a neighbor. Ask a preacher. Hell, even ask the bank teller. We're all more than willing to help each other out when trouble strikes.

That's why I've been able to hold onto my family home. It's been passed down for generations, standing in this same old spot, surrounded by gorgeous rolling farmland far as the eye can see. I work my butt off, but I've also had assistance from friends in the community. Pals of my late father who would sooner go hungry than see Mr. Jensen's daughter in dire straits.

I'm thankful for my job, and I'm grateful to everyone who's helped me out on the way, but lord do I miss having free time. Being happy. Feeling free.

And right now, sitting in the front seat of a handsome stranger's car... well, I'm feeling a rush of that old, forgotten freedom. It's exhilarating. It's frightening. And most of all, it's turning me on. I have never been the kind of girl to blush easy, but something about Alexei just makes my heart flutter. He puts the heat in my body and sends shivers down my spine—but the good kind of shivers. The kind I hope never go away.

I can't help but notice how tiny I feel next to him. My arms, my hands, they seem like the limbs of a doll compared to his thick, muscular arms. His hands gripping the wheel look like they could rip me apart if he so chooses, but I have a feeling he would sooner leap off a cliff than lay a hand on me in anger.

Because for all the power and strength radiating off of him like the glow of the moon, I can't sense even the barest sliver of malice in him. He's a dangerous man. That much I could tell from the first second he sat down next to me at that bar. But it's a danger that thrills me rather than scares me. He's a burning fire, but instead of shying away from the heat, all I want is for those flames to lick me all over and burn me right up.

I glance down at my bare thigh, pale and freckly in the low light as the hems of my sundress and my nightie slip slide up. Next to his tree-trunk body I look frail and fragile. I'm a dandelion under the shade of a mighty oak, but I'd be happy to let him steal my sunshine if that's what he wants.

At least for tonight.

I don't know if it's the late hour or the residual adrenaline from having to escape the likes of Dean Ashcroft hours ago, or maybe it might just be good, old-fashioned sexual magnetism, but I find my mind drifting into dark and dangerous territory. My body yearns for something. Someone.

I want to be bent over and tossed around and folded up into brand new shapes. I want Alexei to make me forget all about Dean and my money troubles and everything else swirling around in my head. I want a distraction, and who better to keep my mind and body entertained than this magnificent, beautiful brute of a man.

Suddenly, that middle cushion between us on the bench seat seems to push me too far away from Alexei. I need to be closer. I need to feel his strength, his warmth. I need to touch him, in however small a way. So I quietly unbuckle my seat belt and scoot over to the middle seat. I click the new seat belt into place and bite my lip, hoping he won't mind my coming closer. His hands tighten on the steering wheel and he glances down at me for a moment, those bright blue eyes flashing. He doesn't push me away, though, and I even get the feeling that he might want me here. Might want me close.

That prospect sends a thrill through my body. To be wanted. What a wild and glorious feeling. And not in the way that Dean wants me. Dean wants to own me, to use and abuse me however he sees fit because he doesn't truly like or respect me. I never should have agreed to go out with him in the first place, but by god, he wore me right down. Coming into the Farm 'n' Feed day in and day out, making eyes at me, waiting around for my shift to end so he could walk me to my truck.

As if there is a single soul in this town I have to fear other than Dean himself. As if he isn't the threat, the coyote wandering in disguise among the flocks.

Oh, he wants me alright. Wants me dead and quiet and obedient. And I just refuse to let a guy like Dean turn me into his idea of a worthwhile woman to court. His desires lead down a dark road and it's not a path I want to follow.

I'm stronger than that.

Smarter.

And I am not desperate enough to let him break me down.

I guess I never quite knew what I wanted up until now. Maybe that's why I've been able to keep hold of my virginity all this time, guarding my heart and my body as though it's a precious secret. As far as I knew, there wasn't a single man in this town worth giving it up to. Most of the men my own age have moved off to college anyway, and the ones left behind are all hicks and party boys. That or they're already married to their high school sweethearts, with a house full of little kids running around like a madhouse.

It's easy to say no when there's nothing tempting on offer. But now? Sitting here next to Alexei, feeling his body so big and strong beside mine? I don't think I can say no even if my life depended on it. For once, I know exactly what I want: I want him. And soon.

I just hope he wants me the same way I want him. I have no doubt in my mind that I'm not the first girl he's danced with at a country bar. The way he spoke to the bartender tells me he's been to the Sugar Creek Tavern before, and who knows how many pretty little things he's plucked out of a bottle and taken home.

But that doesn't matter much to me right now.

I don't need to be his first. I don't need to be his one and only. I just want to be the only one tonight.

"You know," I begin softly, "I don't think I've ever seen you around town."

"I keep to myself," he replies simply.

"I can see that. Not that I get out too much myself, either."

He gives me a rather bemused look.

"A pretty little girl like you doesn't get out much? Now that's either one hell of a lie or a crying shame."

I smile, my heart fluttering again.

"I guess it's a shame, then."

"Well, I'm glad you came out tonight," Alexei says in that sexy, rumbling voice. "I never expected to see such a lovely face sitting at the bar there. You're not exactly the, ah, usual clientele."

I giggle.

"Yeah, this time of night I'm usually tucked up in bed. I guess that makes me sound pretty boring, huh?"

He shakes his head.

"Not at all. Makes you sound responsible. Smart."

"If that's the case, then why are you out tonight?" I ask coyly.

He chuckles gently, a deep vibrating sound that ripples through his body and mine.

"Sometimes a man just needs a good drink, that's all. A drink and some company."

"Am I the kind of company you were expecting tonight?" I inquire, trying to size him up a little better. He smirks and places his hand on my knee, his rough skin feeling so delicious against me. I nearly forget how to breathe.

"Not the kind I was expecting, that's for sure," he answers. "But exactly the kind I was hoping for. Better, actually. I've been in this town for a little while, and I have never seen a woman quite like you."

"You must not go to the Farm 'n' Feed very often, then," I snort. "I work there. Long hours. Sometimes I think I spend more of my waking hours there than at home."

"I buy what I need wholesale," he replies.

"Wholesale?" I repeat, frowning.

He nods slowly.

"Yes. Cut out the middleman."

"And what all are you buying so much of?" I ask. Immediately I worry that I might be infringing on the border of less small talk, more busy bodying.

"Farm supplies. Hay, oats, seeds, meal," he says shortly.

"You're a farmer?" I ask dubiously, raising an eyebrow. "Really?"

"You sound surprised."

I look up at him, smiling, waiting for him to tell me he's just joking. But he doesn't.

"Wait, you're serious?" I press him.

"Yes," he says. "I told you, I run a homestead."

He turns the wheel to the left and we head down a dirt road off the highway, his old truck rumbling over the dirt and rocks. I can tell he's got those tough-as-nails tires on, the kind that can withstand broken glass and whatever the hell else these mean streets have to offer. Maybe he *is* a farmer, after all, I think to myself.

"It's just that… well, you don't seem like the type," I murmur.

As he pulls up beside a big brick-red farmhouse into the wooden carport, he stops the car and takes the key out of the ignition. He turns to me with a knowing look on his handsome face, and again, my breath hitches in my throat.

"Looks can be deceiving, Daisy," he says.

Suddenly, I want him more than ever. I want to give him everything I have. I want him to take me. Maybe if I fall in with this dangerous stranger, Dean will finally back off, leave me alone when he realizes I've been claimed by a far more powerful man.

Or maybe that's just my conscience trying to rationalize my decision to go home with a strange man.

Either way, the conclusion is the same.

"Alexei," I mumble nervously, "I-I want you."

I seize what little spark of courage I have and dive forward, wrapping my arms around him as I press my lips to his. To my relief, he doesn't pull away. He kisses me hard, passionately, his strong hands holding me as I whimper and moan. My whole body is lighting up like a piece of kindling, and I'm willing to burn for him. When he breaks away, he gazes into my face with a hardened look, like he's trying to read my mind.

Then, without a word, he pushes open the door and gives me his hand. He leads me into his farmhouse, our footsteps creaking on the floorboards as we head through the house to his bedroom. His gaze catches mine, his expression unreadable as the seconds stretch out between us.

"You can stay here, if you like. Have the bed."

He's offering me a way out. Letting me know I don't have to do this just for a place to sleep, or maybe even for his protection.

My heart is pounding, but I know what I want.

I start to strip off my dress, but he lays a hand on my shoulder and stops me, shaking his head.

"What's wrong?" I ask, worried.

"I'm going to take care of you," Alexei says emphatically.

I feel a surge of disappointment, thinking that he means he's going to look after me like I'm some little child or something. Like he's just going to heat me up some warm milk and put me to bed.

But then, to my surprise, he scoops me up into his arms and carries me over to the bed, cradling my back before kneeling down between my legs and pushing my dress up. He lifts my legs over his shoulders and hooks a finger under the band of my panties, pulling them aside. I hold my breath, watching wide-eyed as he looks up at me from between my thighs.

ALEXEI

"**D**o you want this?" I ask in a low, husky tone. My cock is thick and hard in my pants, and it's desperate to burst out and claim her. I can see the desire in her eyes, just like she can see it in mine, but I need to hear the words come from her lips.

I pride myself on not being a man like Dean. Not being a man who would ignore the wishes of a woman just to get my rocks off. I might be a trained killer, but I'd never lay a hand on a woman.

"I-I've never done this before," she stammers, her face going redder than it was a moment ago.

I know what that means.

She's a virgin.

My cock swells even stronger, but I don't break my gaze on her for a second. On principle, this doesn't change anything for me. But this is a country girl, someone who has been raised all her life with a certain set of values that are hard to shake.

She should be getting touched like this by a loving husband, someone she believes she has saved herself for and nobody else. That seems to be what most people around here feel, anyway.

To say this is taboo would be an understatement.

I remove my hand from her panties and bring my face up to hers, looming over her and looking down at her with those same, hungry eyes.

"You haven't answered my question," I say slowly, each syllable carrying its weight.

"I…" she hesitates, biting her lip.

"One word, and I'm gone," I say. "That's all it takes. No pressure."

"I want you," she finally breathes, nearly trembling at hearing the words come from her full lips. "I'm just nervous."

"I've got you," I growl, and the words send a shiver through her body as her eyes close and her head tilts back to expose herself to me.

Backing down to her thighs, I reveal her pussy once more, and she squirms in my grasp.

"I told you I'm going to take care of you," I growl, "and I meant it."

The taste of honeysuckle greets my tongue with her heady scent as I pass over her slick lips. She must have been wanting me far longer than I realized to already be so wet, so ready for me. As soon as my tongue hits her, her whole body shudders as the anticipation breaks.

Her hands go to the sides of my head, and she runs her fingers through my hair as she gets a grip on me. I hear her draw in a sharp breath with the stroke, and when I let my tongue out again to do the same thing, her grip tightens on me.

This poor girl is wound tighter than a bowstring just waiting to be plucked.

The tip of my tongue dives deep into her pussy and tastes her sweet honey that has never been tasted before. I wonder if she has ever thought about what this would feel like, having a tongue caressing her pussy like this.

Whatever her expectations, I plan to blow them out of the water.

My tongue takes its time wandering along her flesh, feeling her slick wetness and the heat radiating all around my face. She smells wonderful, and she makes me hungry for more of her. My tongue reaches the end of its journey, and I let the tip slide up to her swollen clit.

The moment I touch her there, it's like I put fire to her. She jolts, her hips thrusting up into me, but I have a firm grip on her. I'm completely in control of the situation, and no matter how she squirms, I have her.

My tongue lingers on her clit and swirls around it, toying with it. She lets out a moan that makes my cock twitch in desire for her, but I'm going to take my time with her pussy against my mouth before I think about that.

I tease her nerves to the point that she starts thrusting her hips up in a soft, steady rhythm, and I move my tongue in time with it until I bring it back down to the bottom of her pussy and dive down again.

Each time I do, I bring more of her honey with me, the wet sound of my feast the only other sound in the room besides her soft moans. She's so unserved, so deserving of release, and each move she makes spurs me on to give that to her.

"Fuck," she groans, and her fingers dig into my hair desperately.

I start stroking her pussy from base to top over and over again, letting our rhythm do the work for us while each stroke seems to edge her closer and closer to the brink. Every now and then, I break the rhythm by lingering at her clit and teasing the nub until she really starts squirming, then I bring my tongue back down into her to start the rhythm up again. This game of edging her closer and closer is better than I could have expected, but she picks up on it before long.

When I bring my tongue to her clit, she tries to push my head down into it, keeping me there, begging for more, but I won't let her have as much as she wants. I'm in control, and I'm going to tease her as long as I want.

She whimpers and pouts when my tongue leaves her once more and slides back up to that bundle of nerves ever so slowly, but this time, I linger a little longer there. In and out, my tongue starts darting faster and faster to and from her clit, and each time I get up there, I spend more time lavishing it with attention.

Finally, after what feels like so long that she must be wound up tighter than ever before, I start to give her what she wants.

I let my tongue stay on her clit, and it starts darting in and out of my mouth, striking it with such precision and rhythm that I hear her gasps get louder and more needy.

"Yes, Alexei, please," she whimpers so pathetically that my heart is moved for her. "Just like that, don't stop!"

I oblige her.

Her hips writhe and squirm harder and harder as I torture that swollen clit, and I feel her whole body welling up in tension.

It almost sounds like she's crying, but when I open my eyes and look up at her while driving her closer to orgasm, I see nothing but anticipation and pleasure on her face. She must not even believe this is happening to her so fast.

Finally, her mouth falls open, and I feel her falling over the precipice of orgasm.

"Ohhhh god!" she cries out, and I feel my face flooded with her sweet honey.

I bury my face in her, using my tongue to take in as much of it as I can while I hold her hips down, letting her feel everything in blissful release without the ability to pull back from it. Her sighs of delight make my cock so thick that it feels like it could burst from my pants.

After a full minute, she goes limp and squeezes her thighs, silently asking for me to pull back, and I do. I raise my wet face and smile down at her as she looks up at me in awe and shock.

"I...I had no idea it would be like that," she breathes. "That was incredible, Alexei."

I come forward and stroke her face with a big hand, letting my thumb run across her lip.

"Your body is beautiful, Daisy. You deserve only the best."

"Please," she whimpers, putting her hand over mine. "I want you inside me, Alexei."

I move my hand to my belt and pause, narrowing my eyes at her.

"Do you?" I ask in a soft, husky voice. "There's no going back from here, Daisy. I'm no kindly farm boy."

"I know," she gasps, "that's why I need you so badly. *Please.*"

She's begging for me, utterly desperate. I've given her some release, but I've had none of my own, and nothing is more tempting than the sweet honey-suckle flower below me. Her legs rest on my muscular shoulders, and a powerful hand still holds her in place, completely in my power. She's all mine, and she wants me.

What she's asking for is a deadly sin.

If only she knew what kind of sinner I am.

I slide my belt off and toss it aside, then unbutton my pants with one hand.

"As you wish," I growl.

She cranes her head to watch me with innocent wonder as I open my pants, and I let my colossal cock spring free.

I hear a sharp gasp of anticipation when she lays eyes on it.

My cock is long and thick, bulging with desire for Daisy and need for release. She can see every inch of it, from the bulging veins that run up and down the thick shaft to the dark crown at the tip to the heavy balls that are swollen with virile seed.

I bring a hand to it and stroke it slowly, and it twitches up in response.

"Be sure that you want this," I say.

"Do you... do you think it will fit?" she asks, genuinely worried, but she reaches down for it with a wary hand. I let her touch it, and it stiffens at her fingertips. She wraps her hand around it and gives it a soft stroke from tip to base, and her face is cherry red. I don't think she's ever seen a cock before, much less stroked a stiff one.

"Yes," I say. "With patience."

She looks up at me, eyes shining with wonder.

"I have a condom," I say, reaching for my back pocket.

"No," she says, shaking her head. "I... I want it the way it is, no birth control," she says with intense confidence.

My heart skips a beat, thinking about defiling that pure, virgin body, unprotected. I'd question if she was thinking straight, but her expression is totally sincere.

I crack a smile and lean forward to press my lips to hers.

Her honey is still on my face, so it's a wet kiss, and it makes it all the sweeter when she sighs into me and moans desperately.

While our lips are together, I put my bulging tip against her soft, ready lips, and she sucks in a sharp breath through her nose and lets her eyes spring open.

Our kiss breaks, and she gives me a quick nod, anticipating my question.

I enter her.

It's a fluid, easy entry, and I feel every inch of her as my crown parts her lips and delves deeper than my tongue ever went, filling her on all sides until she's wrapped tight around half of my cock. I told her I would be careful, and I will.

Her face looked overwhelmed, eyes wide and mouth hanging open. She put her hands up and on my sides, letting them move up and down my hardened abs all the way down to my chiseled hips. Her movements are clumsy and graceless, and it's terribly cute. The poor thing has no idea what to do with herself, faced with such feeling.

I rock back and forth gently at first, sliding out nearly to the tip before pushing back into her. As I do, her eyes go lidded, then closed as she starts to let herself relax and enjoy the feeling.

As for me, my cock feels red-hot and ready to explode at any second, buried deep in her tight womanhood. It is *incredible.*

Of course I had thought about what she might be like. How could I not? She is fire and bliss all at once, and I never knew I could need someone as badly as I now need her. Months without any real contact, and even longer without the touch of a woman, and Daisy is everything I need.

My cock goes a little deeper with each thrust, and as it does, I bring my hands to Daisy's breasts and grope them through her dress. I start working the sundress off her while I thrust. She's a beautifully useless mess under me, completely overwhelmed by what she's feeling. When finally her chest is bare, I watch as her breasts bounce with every thrust of my hips, her nipples stiff and craving my touch.

My hands roam up over her soft skin, gliding between her breasts before I grasp the right one in my hand. I feel its softness while my thumbs and forefingers play with her nipple. It's stiff and swollen, and when I touch it, Daisy gasps, and her eyes spring open.

She looks like she's almost in a dream as I thrust deep into her over and over again. She barely seems aware that her dress has come off, but the sight of me ravishing her body brings out a sigh of joy from her.

I pause to wrap a hand around the back of her neck and kiss her deeply. Our tongues play with each other, going back and forth and enjoying each other's taste. Everything about Daisy is proving to be delicious in more ways than I expected.

This country girl is full of surprises.

I break the kiss and sit almost upright, bringing her legs with me. I start driving down onto her as I pick up the pace of my thrusting. I take her hips in my hands and use them to help me bring her in nearly all the way down my shaft, my heavy balls hitting her ass as I thrust, and my rhythmic grunting starts to fill the room along with her desperate panting.

She grabs the sheets, and I can tell she's about to come again. She looks surprised at the feeling, almost embarrassed—does she not even know that she can come more than once? The thought almost makes me smile sadly as I pound into her, legs wrapped over my shoulders, her whole body moving as I start pistoning into her harder and faster.

"Don't stop," she gasps, the only thing she's able to signal to me. "Alexei, don't stop!" I cup my hand under the small of her back and push her up so that the angle my cock rams into her changes, and I hear her gasp as her whole body goes tense.

The next moment, I feel her wet folds pulse, and I can feel her wetness all over my cock, mixing with the beads of precum that well up at the tip of my thick shaft.

"I told you I would take care of you," I growl as I keep thrusting into her through the whole orgasm, drawing it out and making every single moment electrifyingly sweet for her. My body ripples with muscle that's swollen from the workout we're giving each other, and the burn has never felt sweeter.

I let one of her legs slip from my shoulder to change the angle yet again, fucking her almost sideways as I look down on her exhausted form and realize she can't take much more.

I will be merciful this time.

I let my bucking get less precise and wilder as I take her like a doll and use her, wildly thrusting into parts of her that nobody has gone before, bringing out feelings that not even Daisy realizes she's capable of feeling. She gropes at the sheets and bites down on them as I get wilder, and little by little, I feel the tension unlocking deep inside me, every ounce of masculine energy welling up into this moment.

Daisy makes me feel like a man in ways I haven't felt in a very long time. Living out a quiet farm life is nice, but there's none of the thrill that kept me going in my old life... until now. Until this sweet country girl fell into my arms and offered me her flower.

Her flower. It's an American phrase that I thought silly at first, but it seems apt now.

I let my head fall back as my balls tighten, and I don't hold back from spoiling her pristine little pussy.

Coming inside her with no protection makes it one of the sweetest and most intense orgasms I can ever remember having. My eyes roll back in my head, a growl filling the room as my cock twitches deep within her fertile, young body.

"Oh god!" Daisy cries out as she comes yet again, this time along with me. The first shot of my seed is thick, long, and heavy, and it goes deep inside her, covering her insides. Another comes after it, then another, my whole shaft pulsing with hot energy that Daisy helped bring out of me.

My thick cock empties itself into her while her whole body convulses in her own orgasm, and it feels like it lasts an eternity.

Finally, the pulses stop, and I know I am spent inside her.

I hear our panting, smell our sweat and heady scents in the air, and I look down at her.

Some of my seed rolls down her front from her overflowing pussy, and her blushing face is positively glowing. I crack a smile at her and rub her thighs lovingly.

"God in heaven," she murmurs in that accent I'm coming to love. "Is it always like this?"

I reach down and pinch her ass.

"That's up to you," I growl in a voice still thick with desire. I slowly pull out of her, still stiff, and she whimpers at the feeling. "But me, I am not a man who disappoints."

I lie down beside her, and she instinctively cuddles into me. There's still the smell of alcohol on both our breaths, and we look into each other's glassy eyes as we start to feel the evening's excitement catching up to us in a wonderful, exhausting way.

"You look thoughtful," I say softly. "And beautiful, the way your hair falls over your face on the pillow."

She blushes and turns her head down, laughing, but I grin and wrap an arm around her to pull her into me.

"This is all just a lot, so fast," she says.

"Too fast?"

"No," she says, "and that's what surprises me. I

liked that. A lot." She chews on her lip a moment, then asks, "Can I stay in here tonight? With you?"

I chuckle and hug her tight to me, stroking her hair. "Do you think I'd let you sleep by yourself?" I murmur into her ear.

She lets out a contented sigh, and within minutes, I feel her breathing go into a slow, sleeping rhythm.

I don't last much longer, falling into the best sleep I've had in years soon after.

...and when I open my eyes to the soft light of the morning sun, my bed is empty.

DAISY

The sweet light of dawn comes streaming in through the square window above the kitchen sink, casting the room with a thick pillar of golden sunshine. I yawn and stretch, feeling warm and cozy in my panties and the oversized t-shirt I lifted from Alexei's closet to put on, despite the butterflies still flitting around in my stomach.

I am amazed at how relaxed and happy I feel, how glad I am to have given myself up to Alexei last night. When I first woke up in the early, pale hours this morning, I was a little afraid. This is all-new territory for me, and waking up next to a huge, powerful, sleeping giant is not something I ever imagined would happen to me, not even in my sweetest fantasies. Of course, these days I don't have much time for fantasy. The duties and trappings and minutiae of real life bog me down so much that by the end of a long day I hardly have enough energy left to cook dinner and get ready for bed, much less to dream.

I know what they say, that everyone dreams every night. But I scarcely remember them, and when I do, it's not something I want to remember. From time to time I have nightmares. About the house burning down. Losing my job. Wrecking the truck. And of course, that most painful reenactment of watching my father pass away. Still, the dreams in which Daddy is still alive are a thousand times worse than the ones in which he dies. Because I always wake up smiling and relieved, until my memories catch up to me and remind me with a jolt of pain that he's not here, that it is just a dream.

But this morning, I don't feel that pain quite so sharply as I usually do. I feel refreshed and renewed. It's like that feeling of lying down on freshly-laundered sheets after a long day at work. Like that first sip of hot brewed coffee when you're exhausted and weak.

Alexei is like a shot of adrenaline to my heart, but at the same time, he's like a pillow under my head. He excites me and calms me at the same time. I don't understand how that can be possible, but here it is. And now I want to return the favor, in however small a way I can manage. That's why I sneaked out of his bed and tiptoed across the house to the kitchen. I plan on cooking him a big, hearty breakfast. I only hope I can get it done before he wakes up and ruins the surprise.

I walk over to the fridge and softly pull it open, squinting and squatting down to see what ingredients I have to choose from. I have seen in movies and read in magazines that most men are useless in the kitchen. Lord knows my father was. Being raised by him, I grew up eating a lot of boxed macaroni and cheese and chopped-up hot dogs. A lot of takeout from our favorite local restaurant, Maud's Diner. Pretty much as soon as I was tall enough to reach the stove, I became the chef in the house. I borrowed cookbooks from the tiny community library, photocopying recipes using the printer there. Daddy was uptight about my Internet use back then, but he relented when he realized that most of my Internet time was spent perusing cooking blogs for more ideas. He benefited directly from that, so he gave me a little more freedom.

Nowadays, I consider myself a pretty damn good cook, although I work so much that I hardly have the time or occasion to cook. It's difficult and a little sad just cooking for one, especially since I still naturally gravitate toward cooking enough for Daddy and myself.

I smile when I realize that Alexei's refrigerator is much better-stocked than even my own. He has all the accoutrements of a hearty breakfast worthy of an amazingly-powerful body like his, and I plan on pulling out all the stops.

I take out a package of thick-cut bacon— not the grocery store stuff, either. It clearly comes from the local butcher shop. And then I grab some eggs in a ceramic carton. They're all different shapes and colors, with some tiny feathers still attached to them. This makes me grin, the image of that huge, imposing guy stooping down to care for those silly, clucking birds endlessly entertaining to me. I wonder if he's given them names. The thought is almost too precious to bear.

Almost as though they could hear my thoughts, I hear a rooster crowing from far away. I clap a hand over my mouth as I start giggling, then force myself to be serious again. I take out a loaf of protein bread and chop up some red potatoes I find in the pantry, along with onions and peppers from the produce rack in the corner. *He must be one hell of a cook to have all these fresh ingredients on hand,* I think to myself.

I start frying up the bacon, listening to it crackle and sizzle on the hot pan. As it's cooking, I stand with my hand on my hip, peering out the kitchen window. Outside, I can see a grand expanse of green fields with wooden fences and the occasional fruit tree. If I squint, I can make out a chicken coop to one side. In the distance, I see what looks to be a horse stable, and that makes my heart leap with joy. I have always loved horses, ever since I was a little girl, but Daddy and I never had enough money to rub together to buy one for ourselves.

Besides, our place doesn't have the acreage. But I grew up riding horses that belonged to our friends and neighbors, and it's been my dream to have my own horse someday. Well, now that I'm adult with a busy life and a shoestring budget, that little dream has been deferred.

When the bacon is finished, I set it aside to dry and cool while I fry the potatoes, onions, and peppers in the fat, seasoning as I go. I pop two slices of toast into the toaster and start whipping up the eggs. While I stand over the stove, it hits me how blissful and right this feels.

Cooking for a good man, caring for him, making sure he has what he needs. I might as well be a fifties housewife right now. Just hang an apron on me and call me Betty Crocker. Not that I would ever be the kind of girl to just cook and clean and have no life of her own. I'm not a housewife. I'm an independent, hard-working young woman. But sometimes it can feel pretty damn good playing house like this. I love cooking. I love being in the kitchen, but only because it's what *I* want, what *I* like.

Oh, go ahead and tell yourself that, I think to myself wryly. I laugh softly and roll my eyes. There's no need to overthink this situation. I'm just a happy girl cooking breakfast for a good man who picked me up when I was down and gave me one hell of a great night. Nothing more, nothing less.

Still, there is that small voice in the back of my mind warning me, telling me that I might be stepping out of line here. That I might be allowing my feelings to take over and ignore my better judgment.

I don't really know this man. We have only spent one night together, and for part of it, I was tipsy. But I can't rationalize the way I feel when I'm around him. That goes far beyond the realm of scientific explanation. It's not something I can really put into words. It's just a feeling, a little spark between us that I hope he can sense, too.

Even if he probably can't feel it with the same intensity that I do.

He makes me feel safe. Protected. Alexei's presence gives me confidence and tells me that maybe, just maybe, everything will work out alright. After all, I started out last night climbing out of my own bathroom window and bolting across the yard to escape the wrath of one dangerous man. And by the end of the night, I ended up safe and blissful in the arms of a second dangerous man, only this one seems to truly respect me. At least, I hope he does. That nagging voice smugly sneers that he might have respected me up until the point when I went to bed with him even though we were total strangers.

But I don't think Alexei thinks that way. He didn't treat me like some flavorless conquest. He touched me and kissed me and moved me like I was something more. Like I mean something more to him than just a random roll in the hay.

As I'm pouring two glasses of orange juice and plating up our meal, I hear Alexei's heavy footsteps getting louder and closer. My heart starts pounding and I hastily wash my hands and face in the kitchen sink, drying myself off as he walks into the room. I smile at him, drinking in his intimidating height and strength.

He's shirtless, wearing just a pair of sweatpants which do nothing at all to hide the noticeable bulge of his cock. His chest and shoulders are so broad and muscular it makes my eyes widen. I mean, I knew what he looked like last night, but there's something to be said about seeing him in the bright light of day. He looks like he could snap me in half without even trying.

I know that should frighten me, but instead, it just turns me on and makes me feel safer. I wonder if that means there's something wrong with me.

Alexei looks around at the impressive breakfast spread on the table, then glances up at me with an amused expression.

"Well, good morning," he says in that rough, growly voice I'm starting to love so much.

"Good morning." I reply brightly. "I just thought that after... last night... it might be a good idea for us to get a good, hearty breakfast and replenish all those calories we burned."

He chuckles as he slowly saunters over to me. He puts his strong arms around me and pulls me close, kissing the top of my head, my cheeks, my neck, my shoulders. Before long I'm sighing and whimpering, limp and soft as putty in his hands.

"You're one hell of a woman. I cannot think of a single better way to wake up in the morning," he rumbles, cupping my face as those blue eyes pierce into my soul. "Well, except for what I would have done for you had you not rushed off to give me this delicious surprise."

I bite my lip, hoping he can't hear the way my heart is galloping along like a startled doe. I can feel my cheeks flushing pink, every cell in my body responding to his touch with added heat.

"You're welcome," I say in a small voice. "We should eat before it gets cold."

"Agreed," he replies, letting go of me and taking a seat at the table. I sit down across from him, still tingly and on fire from just being close to him. It's hitting me now how crazy it was for me to ever think I was attracted to Dean Ashcroft. Hell, even before he showed his true colors and turned into a dangerous, creepy stalker, I never felt even one-tenth of the sparks I feel when I'm with Alexei.

This, I realize, is what true attraction feels like. I can only hope that he feels the same way I do.

Judging from the way he looks at me, I think there might be a chance.

"How is it?" I ask, peering at his plate.

He looks up at me with an appreciative nod.

"Fantastic. It's been a while since I've have a good, home-cooked meal."

I frown in confusion, tilting my head to one side.

"But you had all of these awesome ingredients on hand. Don't take this the wrong way, but your kitchen seems like it should belong to a man who cooks all the time."

"Well, that's been my intention. Occasionally I find the time to eat something substantial, but I spend most of my hours working. I can cook but not very well," he admits.

"Oh," I reply simply. I take a bite of bacon and eggs and then continue a little cautiously, "Have you lived here very long? Not to pry or anything, but Broken Pine is a pretty small town. Most of us who live here have been here for years. Decades. My dad's family has owned the same property since the turn of the last century. I know just about everybody by now, or at least I can recognize their faces."

Alexei sets down his fork, but doesn't look up.

"I have not been here very long. But long enough to know that this town is a safe haven. This little patch of country is a refuge. It's off the beaten path, and I can tell that not too many travelers pass through here. But to me, it's the most desirable point on the map."

I blink in surprise.

"Really? Broken Pine?" I wrinkle my nose.

He raises his eyes to meet my gaze, and there's a stillness, a quiet fire burning there. I feel a shiver tremble down my spine.

"Yes," he says with a nod. "For a weary man who wants to slow down and live quietly, there is no better place."

"Where did you come here from? After Russia, I mean," I ask.

Alexei looks away again.

"New York City." He picks up his fork and keeps eating as I gawk at him in total awe.

"New York? Really?" I gasp. "I've always dreamed of seeing New York City. But why? Why would you leave a place like that to come to a place like this? I mean, don't get me wrong, Broken Pine is my home and it has its charms. But I can't imagine leaving the big city behind to move all the way out here."

"I needed a change of pace," he says.

I lean forward, unable to control my interest.

"What was it like there? The city that never sleeps! I bet it was amazing."

"It's noisy," he answers, "and filthy."

"Oh," I say, a little put out.

He tempers the mood with a smile.

"Like you said, it has its charms. But I grew tired

of them. I wanted something different. Quieter. More peaceful."

"Here everybody knows each other. The houses are spread far apart, but we still treat everyone like a neighbor," I muse aloud. "It must be strange getting used to that, coming from a city where you can blend in. Where you can be anonymous. Just a face in the crowd."

"Even in a city that large, it's impossible to disappear. There are always people who know how to find you, no matter how quiet you are and how elaborate your disguise is," Alexei says in a low voice. Something about his cryptic words gives me an ominous feeling in the pit of my stomach. Like there's something more he's not saying. A lot more.

But I'm distracted from the conversation by the sound of my cell phone chiming from the other room. "Oh, excuse me for a moment. That might be my boss or something," I tell him, hastily getting up to go grab it. I walk into the bedroom and grab my phone from the dresser. I slide the screen open to see a new text message, but to my horror it's not from my boss.

It's from Dean.

I saw you go home with him last night, you little slut. If you think Mr. Tall Dark and Handsome can keep you safe from me, you're dead wrong. I'm coming for you, and nobody on this planet can stop me.

ALEXEI

*T*he terrified gasp that comes from the bedroom tells me everything I need to know about the message Daisy just got, and I feel my muscles tense. Immediately, I follow in after her and find her standing there with a hand to her mouth, looking wide-eyed at the phone.

When she realizes I'm there, she tries to pretend like nothing is wrong, but she soon realizes I can read the situation too well.

"What is it?" I ask, stepping forward.

"I…" she trails off, trying to turn away from me, but I don't plan on letting her act like whatever she's looking at isn't a big deal. I hold out my hand with a grave expression, and she's hesitant at first, but she hands me the phone before sitting down on the bed and staring at the ground vacantly.

I read the message, and my face goes ashen.

How *dare* this sadistic hick think he can threaten a woman like that, much less this one.

I read over the text one more time, making sure I haven't missed out on anything and that it is truly from Dean. But there can be no mistake. I knew it in my gut the moment I watched Daisy reading it.

I turn the screen off and toss the phone onto the bed, and Daisy looks up and meets the icy gaze I'm giving her.

"I'll take care of this," I say.

Every word has deadly weight to it. She looks up at me with those big, innocent, hazel eyes, and I can see every drop of fear and worry in that gaze.

"What do you mean?"

I put a hand on her shoulder and give it a reassuring squeeze. "You've been through more than enough, Daisy, and the people of Broken Pine clearly aren't doing their job watching out for one of their own. I can't stand by and watch this go on."

I walk to the drawer and pull out a towel, along with one of my bathrobes. It's comically too big for Daisy's small frame, and when I hand her the armful of fabric, she looks like she's holding an entire blanket, blinking up at me in confusion.

"My bathroom is spacious, and the tub is quite comfortable," I say in a calm, even tone. "Let's put plans for the day on hold for now. Go enjoy a bath and take your mind off this."

"I don't want to have someone else feeling like

they need to fight my battles for me, Alexei," she says, but that fear in her eyes tells me how desperately she needs a hand where none have been offered.

"I understand," I say. "But you want this problem to go away, yes?"

Her lip quivers a moment, and she nods her head. "Yes."

"I will take care of this," I say again, this time in more of a reassuring tone, despite the dark weight the words carry.

She nods, opens her mouth to speak again, then loses the words in her throat. She gives me a feeble, nervous smile, then makes her way into the bathroom and closes the door behind her.

I turn and walk out of the bedroom and make my way down the hall to a closet. Opening it, it looks like an ordinary little room with space for a few brooms propped up against the wall and a vacuum cleaner.

I flick the little lightbulb on and close the door behind me, then reach up and push the top shelf up.

It activates the mechanism that makes the fake back wall come off its secure locks, and I gently, silently push it back and slide it to the side. Slowly, I lock the closet door behind me and step inside the room I worked so hard to keep hidden.

It is a room that I hoped I would never have to step into again.

With a flick of another switch, lights come on in the long, soundproof room, illuminating the racks upon racks of guns I have lined up on display.

I have more pistols than I know what to do with, three assault rifles, two sniper rifles, a small stock of fragmentation grenades, enough knives to arm the town of Broken Pine, and a stock of clothes more suitable for moving through the shadows.

My private arsenal is such that if the mafia I used to work for comes looking for me out here in the middle of nowhere, I can hold my own. It would take a small army to take me down, if I had enough time to know it was coming for me.

But today, I knew that I have to carry out a very different job.

Today, I need to carry out a job not unlike the ones I did for so long, trading stunning amounts of money for taking human lives. I was a hunter of men back then, a force in the shadows who did the bidding of murderers. There is blood on my hands from my past. More blood than I can justify.

Getting away from all that is why I came out here to Broken Pine in the first place. But it seems that I will carry that life with me wherever I go.

I take a single pistol from the arsenal and begin to clean it, making sure it's in working order. This pistol has a special sentimental value to me. It is the first weapon that was entrusted to me when I set foot in the United States so long ago as an enforcer for the Bratva.

The humble Makarov pistol is in as good a condition as I could hope for, and I pull on a pair of black gloves before loading it and placing it into a little black bag along with its suppressor.

But I still hold out some hope that I won't have to use it.

I move to a safe at the far end of the room and turn the dial until I hear a click, and I swing the heavy door open.

Inside are stacks upon stacks of cash.

This is my emergency fund—just shy of a million, stashed away over the years thanks to several high-profile assassinations. I have more than this in my accounts, but this is something I've been saving for a rainy day. I won't even need to put a dent in it for what I plan to do today.

I withdraw about $20,000 from the pile and place it in the black bag along with my gun and a few other tools I use for these kinds of operations. With nothing but my usual outfit, gloves, and my bag, I head out of the room and seal it behind me, listening at the door of the closet before opening it and stepping back out into my house.

I hear the sound of bathwater running from my bedroom, and I take a deep breath. She listened to me. Good.

With a final look to the bathroom door, thinking

of that innocent face, I silently make my way out the door and head to my truck.

I put the bag behind the passenger's seat and take out a device I have stored under the driver's seat.

It's a GPS tracker.

When I left the bar with Daisy last night, I didn't go straight to my truck and take us home. I put Daisy in the passenger's seat and told her that I had to check on something in the bed of the truck, muttering something about a towel I forgot back there.

In reality, I grabbed a GPS tracker while she wasn't looking, then slipped into the parking lot. It was all over in less than a minute.

I found Dean's truck in no time. I recognized the truck from the store, and I saw a bumper sticker on the back—it was a little picture of James Dean, the rebel without a cause. The thought that Dean had taken to calling himself that was laughable. The sticker was just above and to the left of a tacky pair of truck nuts hanging below the license plate. I stuck the tracker under the truck just in case of something like this.

I did it to protect her. From the moment I saw the look on Dean's face when he saw us leaving together, I knew this problem wouldn't go away on its own.

Sometimes, I hate being right.

The tracker shows Dean's position at a diner in town. It must be his day off.

I can't deal with him there, so I pull out of the driveway and start heading into town more slowly than usual, keeping an eye on the tracker as I go.

For the next hour, I waste time driving around the country roads, waiting. This is the hunter's game. It's strange—this is hardly the kind of setting one would expect a hitman to be doing his work. The sun is shining, and the smell of hay and fresh earth is in the air. As I drive by some of my neighbors, they give me a courtesy wave from their drivers' seats, and I return them, as always.

Everything about the day is idyllic, except for the rolling gray clouds coming in from the west. The wind picks up, and it starts pushing the ominous clouds closer to town. It will be raining heavily soon, if my instincts are right.

Good.

Finally, I see the tracker start to change positions. Dean's lunch is over, and he's on the move again.

I watch the little dot on the screen heading out the opposite side of town down a long, empty road toward the closest thing this town has to a neighborhood on the outskirts. Country "neighborhoods" tend to be made of a smattering of houses along long stretches of road with a lot of space between each one. If your yard isn't at least an acre out here, then something is wrong.

I start heading his way, and when I'm about halfway through town, I see the tracker come to a stop at a house. He might be home, but it could be a friend's house just as easily, so I take it slowly and keep watching.

To my surprise, I see him start to move again soon, heading further down the rows of side-roads and houses.

This makes me curious.

I drive toward the first place he stopped, and I see a long gravel driveway leading to a cozy country house that looks like a patch of paradise. There's a mailbox at the front of the driveway, and hanging from it is a little sign with a name painted on it in white paint.

Jenson.

It's Daisy's house.

Immediately, I feel my blood boiling. Dean stopped by Daisy's house to see if she was home. If she had been, there's no telling what would have happened today. Any reservations I had left over about dealing swiftly and harshly with Dean evaporate, and my grip on the steering wheel tightens.

I check my GPS again. Dean's signal has stopped at another house a few miles away.

I put my truck into gear and roar after him.

Before long, I find myself slowing down and driving by a shoddy-looking bungalow at the end of a dirt path, up against some woods and brush. The yard isn't maintained at all, and there are even a few car parts not far from a rotting wooden carport.

Dean's truck is parked there, and nobody else's.

There's nobody on the road as far as the eye can see in front or behind me, and because of how much open space there is out here, it's difficult to sneak up on anyone—but that won't be necessary today. Not with what I have planned.

As I hear thunder start to rumble overhead, the gray clouds casting a shadow over everything now, I pull down the driveway, but instead of pulling up beside Dean's truck, I bring mine around the back. There's a little space between the back of the house and the woods, and in those woods, I see a dirt trail with truck tracks on it. I make a mental note to use that way to make my exit, whatever happens here.

I bring my vehicle to a stop almost right up against the back of the house. He knows I'm here, there's no doubt about that. And that's just fine.

I quickly put my suppressor on my pistol and tuck it into my jeans behind me, grab the bag, and make my way toward the back door.

I see Dean's face at the kitchen window as I approach, and he quickly moves to the door to yank it open as I reach it.

"*You?* Your Russky ass had better have a good goddamn reason to be here, or I'll-"

My fist flashes up faster than he can react, and my knuckles catch him in the nose, sending him staggering back and clutching his face. I hear rain start to pour on the house just as he cries out in pain and opens his eyes to glare at me as he takes his hands from his face, blood trickling down his nose.

"You fucked with the wrong guy, you son of a bitch," he snarls, and he puts his fists up, but I put a hand up instead.

"That was just for the cow you tortured," I say calmly. "I'm here to discuss Daisy."

His jaw tightens, and he doesn't lower his fists, but he doesn't lunge at me, either. For a split second, I notice his eyes dart to a corner of the kitchen behind me. If I know these country people by now, I'm sure there's a shotgun leaning in that corner that he wants to get to. If it comes to that, I won't let that happen.

"Don't got nothin' to discuss," he says. "Come in here and pop a cheap shot on a man on his own property, and you want to *talk* about it? Ha! It's none of your fucking business, understand?"

"*Talk* might have been the wrong word," I say with a cold smile. "How about *tell*?"

I set the black bag on the counter, and I pop the buttons open and open it slowly and deliberately, wide enough that he can see the piles of cash inside.

If there's one thing that will get his attention, it's that, and he proves me right. His eyes go wide at what he sees, and he looks at me in complete bewilderment.

"What the fuck is this?" he growls.

"This," I say, "is yours, if you're smart. I'm here because you're a piece of shit, Dean, and Broken Pine would be a better place without you. The way you've been carrying on with Daisy is unacceptable."

"She's my girl, you chickenshit," he snarls. "And you got no right comin' in here and playing home-wrecker!"

"There's no home to wreck, Dean," I say. "You're fooling yourself. She doesn't want you."

"Probably because your commie ass has been planting lies in her head!" he snaps, but I just tap the bag of money to get his attention again.

"This is $20,000 in untraceable cash," I say. "Here's what's going to happen. You're going to take that bag as a gift from me to you. You're going to get in your truck, and you're going to drive far, far away, out of state, and start a new life for yourself. Neither Daisy nor I will hear from you as long as we all live. You don't have a lot of brain cells left, but surely that must sound good even to you."

He scoffs, and a smile crosses his dull face.

"I got a better idea. I take that cash *and* Daisy on a little trip while your stupid-ass is recovering in the hospital."

He throws a punch at me.

I catch it.

He looks stunned as I stand there, holding his fist in my hand almost effortlessly. He's my size and build, but he doesn't have the kind of experience I have controlling his body and fighting in hand-to-hand combat.

I crack a smile.

"I was hoping you'd say that."

I bring my fist into his stomach, and he coughs as I knock him back and release him. The next second, he rushes past me to dive for the shotgun that is indeed leaning in the corner of the kitchen.

He has sealed his fate.

In a fluid motion, I reach for my pistol, pull it out, and aim it at the back of his head.

Thunk.

Dean's blood and flecks of brain land on the shotgun, and his body goes limp next to it, dead.

It's done.

I hold my pistol out, still as a statue, watching the body to make sure it's truly dead. I watch a trickle of splattered blood on the wall run down to the floor not far from his vacant, staring eye.

Finally, I lower my weapon and slide the bag over to me. I push the money aside to start calmly taking out the cleaning tools I packed with me, preparing to clean up the scene of the murder without missing a beat.

It's all instinct for me. The killing instinct is one that will never leave me, until the day I die. I know this to be true, and this just proves it yet again.

I'd walked away from that life, from everyone

who'd ever hired me to kill for them, from everyone who ever knew who and what I was. I wanted a fresh start.

But Daisy is a woman worth killing for.

I stoop down over Dean's body to start doing the dark work that I'm so well versed in, and my hands move with practiced ease. I don't even have to think about it as I clean the blood off the walls, bit by bit removing all traces that I've been here. I take my time and work with the careful diligence needed to truly get away with murder.

But not even a half hour passes before I hear the crunch of gravel outside of someone approaching.

DAISY

I sit on the edge of the slick, porcelain clawfoot tub, wrapped up in the over-sized robe Alexei let me borrow. I'm watching the hot water come steaming out of the faucet, filling the tub slowly. I can't actually remember the last time I even took a bath. Probably not since I was a child, being washed and cared for by my father. These days I rarely had the time to even take a leisurely shower, much less wallow around in a bubble bath.

In fact, today I should be at work.

But something about the way Dean Ashcroft worded his threat to me makes me wary of even looking out the window. If he knows I went home with Alexei then who's to say he didn't follow us home? He probably knows where I am.

I remember with a jolt that my trusty old truck is

still parked out back behind the Sugar Creek Tavern in that gravel lot. I hope it doesn't get towed.

I stand up and walk to the bathroom counter to pick up my cell phone. If I am going to spend my day holed up in Alexei's farmhouse, I have some important calls to make. First, I dial the number for my boss's desk phone and listen to it ring three times before she picks up.

"Hello, Farm 'n' Feed managerial desk, my name is Jolene. How can I help you?" she rattles off in a cheery, if a little bored tone. I can hear the other phones ringing in the background along with the beep-beep of the cash registers on the other end of the store.

I realize that I need some kind of proper excuse, and force myself to choke out a few nasty-sounding coughs.

"Hi, Miss Jolene. It's Daisy."

"Oh, hey sweetheart! Goodness me, that cough sounds awfully painful," she says with genuine concern. I wince, feeling like a complete jerk for lying to her. Jolene has always been especially kind and patient with me, regarding me almost more like a surrogate daughter or little sister than a lowly employee. Especially since she and my father went to high school together.

Jolene and her wife Harriet, who runs Maud's Cafe, stepped up to the plate after he passed, bringing me all kinds of casseroles and dishes to

I HIRED A HITMAN

help me survive the first few hellish weeks of grief and loss. Jolene is the kind of lady who would bend over backwards to help her friends, and I'm eternally grateful to work for her. Which is why it's extra terrible for me to lie to her right now, but it needs to be done.

"Yes, ma'am," I croak, forcing a few more hacking coughs from my throat. "Feels like I might be coming down with something."

"You got a fever?" she asks. I can just picture her kindly face, frowning with worry.

"Oh, I don't know. I-I don't own a thermometer or anything," I reply quickly.

"Well, honey, first of all, you need to get yourself a thermometer. Everyone should have one of those at home. Second of all, you need to stay home today and look after yourself, okay? What shift do I have you scheduled for again?" she inquires. I can hear her shuffling through papers on her desk, searching for the schedule.

"One to nine-thirty," I answer, taking care to make my voice sound rough.

"Ah, yes. Of course. Well, don't you worry. I'll have Robin take over your shifts today and tomorrow. You work too hard as it is, honey. I know, because I'm the one who makes your schedule. I keep tellin' you, if you don't slow down and watch yourself, you're gonna get all burned out by the time you're twenty-five! You're far too young to be cooped up here at the Farm 'n' Feed all day. Don't get me wrong, sweetie, you're quite possibly my favorite employee— don't tell Archie I said that— but I don't want you gettin' sick because you run yourself ragged, you know?" she says. I can see her clearly in my mind's eye, leaning against the corner of her desk with her arms crossed and the phone pinned between her cheek and shoulder.

"Mhm. Yes, ma'am," I answer.

"I can't be responsible for you ending up in a hospital cot hooked up to a bunch of IVs and what-not. Your daddy would be rollin' in his grave. You know what he told me one time years ago? Back when he first got sick?" Jolene continues.

I smile to myself. She must have told me this anecdote a thousand times.

She answers herself before I even get the chance to say anything.

"He comes to me and he tells me, he says, 'Miss Jolene, you've always been a good friend and a stand-up lady, and if anything were to happen to me, I hope the good people of this town would step up and look after my little girl. Would ya please?' And you know what I told him?"

"Hmm?" I prompted, adding a little cough for emphasis.

"I told your daddy I would do anything for him and his kin. He was good people, your daddy. And so are you. So take it easy today, honey," she orders. I just know she's wiggling her pointer finger at me in her office right now.

I'm grinning by now, even though it hurts my heart to make up an excuse like this to a woman like Jolene who has been nothing but kind to me.

"Yes, ma'am. Will do," I tell her.

"You'd better! Stay in bed, watch some TV, read a book. And don't forget to eat! And if you don't have nothin' at home to eat, don't you hesitate to call up Miss Harriet over at Maud's. She'll bring you over some of her famous chicken noodle soup and a biscuit in a heartbeat," she adds. "In fact, if you'd like, I can go ahead and call her after we hang up—"

"No!" I protest hastily, then temper my outburst with a cough and a softer, "No, thank you. I've got plenty of food here… at home. I'm good, thanks. But tell Miss Harriet I said hi."

"Well, alright, honey. If you say so. I'll let you go get some rest, okay? And if you need anything, anything at all, feel free to give me a holler," Jolene says.

"Okay. I will. Thanks again, Miss Jolene," I tell her.

"Bye, now."

"Bye," I say, hanging up with a heavy sigh.

I feel like I might be bound for hell after lying flat-out to my boss, but she seems to have taken it well. I smile to myself and walk over to the tub to turn off the water as it's already reaching the upper brim. I think to myself how nice it is having a manager who genuinely cares about me. As much as I could complain about Broken Pine and its lack of things to do and places to go, I have to admit that there are certainly charms to living in such a small town.

Especially having grown up here.

Knowing everybody in town can be a double-edged sword: the rumor mill never stops churning and there's no such thing as going out and not running into someone you know. That can be a bad thing if you're not in the mood for a chit-chat, but it sure pays off in situations like this.

I sweep my long, strawberry-blonde hair back into a messy bun, take off the robe and drape it across the bathroom counter, then slip into the bathtub, sighing with pleasure as the hot water envelops my bare body.

I sink down until the water is lapping at my chin, my knees bent out of the soapy water. The whole bathroom smells like the strawberry-scented soap I squirted into the stream of water, making tiny popping bubbles surround me. I close my eyes for a moment, but then remember with a groan that I have another call to make. I sit up and grab the phone from its spot on the bathroom floor. I look up the number for the Tavern and call it, hoping that someone will be there to answer this early in the day. I don't know what time they open, but I hope somebody will be there prepping for the day's shifts.

The line only rings twice before a deep male voice answers.

"Sugar Creek, this is Bill."

"Hi, uh, this is a weird question, but last night I parked my truck in your lot, and then I went home with… someone else. In their vehicle. And I'm just wondering if my truck might still be there or if it got towed or something," I ask, flushing brightly. I feel so awkward admitting to this stranger that I went home with someone from a bar.

"You the owner of that dusty blue truck?" he grunts.

"Yes. The antique one. That's mine," I answer.

"Didn't that used to be Saul Jensen's old truck?" the man asks, a little suspiciously.

"Yes, sir. That was my dad. I'm Daisy Jensen," I tell him.

I can almost hear the change in his facial expression. In a much lighter tone, he says, "Right, yeah. That makes sense. I'd recognize that old clunker anywhere. Your daddy was mighty proud of that truck. Yes, Miss Daisy, your truck is still parked out back. We won't tow it or anything. Don't you worry about that. Redd and I would rather you leave your vehicle here overnight than drive drunk. Did you make it home okay last night? Someone give you a ride?"

I smile, feeling the same rush of warmth and relief I felt before when I was talking to Jolene. Everybody knows me as soon as I tell them I'm Saul Jensen's kid. Suddenly, I'm not a stranger, I'm everybody's favorite southern belle.

I send a silent note of thanks to my father's memory. He was such a wonderful stand-up guy that his good reputation has passed down to me. And in a town this size, reputation is everything. History is everything. It's all about who you know and who you're related to.

"Yes, sir. A, uh, good friend drove me home. I'm safe. I'm feelin' a little under the weather, though. I might not be able to come get my truck right away. Is that alright?" I ask.

"Sure, sure. Of course. We'll hold onto it for you and make sure nobody so much as touches it. Come and get it whenever you're ready. And feel better, you hear?"

"Will do. Thank you, Bill," I say, beaming happily.

"Have a good one, Miss Daisy."

"Bye," I say. I hang up and sit there for a moment just basking in the warmth of that interaction. It's such a sunny, sweet moment that I almost forget all about the worry…

But not completely. The paranoia comes trickling back to me. What the hell is Alexei doing out there in the world right now? He said he would handle it. He would take care of it. But what does that mean in reality? Is he planning some kind of retaliation on Dean Ashcroft?

The thought makes me feel sick to my stomach. Dean may seem like a regular old run-of-the-mill country boy, but I know better than anyone that he's not to be messed with. Like most men around these parts, he's got a healthy collection of guns and rifles. Just about everyone I know goes hunting for sport and to help feed their families, but Dean… well, I don't think Dean is much of an outdoorsman. He just collects weapons because he likes to feel and look tough. He's all about that bad boy image, even though he acts just like a sweet country charmer when he's in mixed company.

But around me?

He's a different man altogether.

I jump a little with fear and surprise when I hear the distinctive crackle of thunder overhead. I glance up at the bathroom window and see, even from this low angle, that the tree branches are shaking and waving in the fierce winds. The weather has turned foul all of a sudden, which isn't much of a shock. Out here on the prairie, the weather has a mercurial temper. One moment, it's blue skies without a cloud in sight. The next moment, there's lightning splitting the sky and it's raining cats and dogs. The rain starts instantly, pounding on the window pane as the wind whistles and howls outside.

I have no doubts that Alexei is a tough guy in his

own right, but he seems so gentlemanly and kind. He's strong and powerful. That much I can tell. But he's got a softness to him. At least, that's what he showed me last night. Plus, he's from the big city. That means he's probably more likely to underestimate a backwoods nobody like Dean.

And Dean should never be underestimated, not in my experience.

It occurs to me, though, that I don't really know quite enough about Alexei to make any truly reasonable assumptions about him or his character. For all I know, he could be a secret agent. Or an axe murderer. Although, the fact that he left me here in his home to take a luxurious bubble bath kind of makes me think the latter guess might be a little off. Besides, why would a truly dangerous, powerful man ever want to leave the glitz and glamor of the big city to come slum it out here in the Midwest countryside?

I reach for my phone again, my heart hammering away as an idea occurs to me. I pull up a couple different social media apps on my phone and type Alexei's name into the search bar. I don't know his last name yet, but I figure how many 'Alexeis' can there really be in America?

As it turns out, there are many more of them than I expected. However, no matter how long I scroll and how many photo galleries I sift through, I never manage to turn up a single guy who looks like he could be my Alexei. And certainly none of them come up under my related search for Broken Pine. He's the first of his name, it seems, possibly ever, to come here. And it doesn't appear that he has any social media presence at all whatsoever.

I have to admit that this realization does set off some alarm bells for me. After all, it's 2018— what person under the age of forty doesn't have some kind of social media account these days? Unless maybe he's one of those off-the-grid folks who think they're too good for social media.

Or maybe… his name isn't actually Alexei.

That option sounds ridiculous to me, though. What reason would he ever have to lie to me? I don't know a single damn thing about him. He could tell me his real name and it wouldn't make a difference. Unless he's a famous person and Alexei is just his alias. But again, why would a famous person ever want to come to a middle-of-nowhere town like Broken Pine? And why would a famous person want to go home with a boring country girl like me?

"Maybe he's done something terrible, and he fled to the countryside to be anonymous and blend in, shake the cops or his enemies off his trail," I mumble to myself, rolling my eyes at the thought. *You're over-thinking this*, I tell myself, *he's not like Dean.*

Finally, I decide to try another search, this time just in a search engine instead of on a social media app. I look up "Alexei New York City."

And to my horror, the first result is a link to a news article about a court proceeding. Before I click it, I keep scrolling to see if there's anything else of note. But no, there seems to be no other mention of Alexei on the internet at all, which is bizarre. So, without any better option, I select the top result and open the link.

It takes me to a news site, recounting a grisly murder trial in New York City from a few years ago. A man named Alexei under fire for second degree murder. I read on to see that the man in custody was acquitted because the witnesses called to the stand all refused to testify.

I frown at the webpage.

How odd. The description of the man on trial is relatively vague, only giving a name, Alexei Niko-laev, and the adjectives *tall*, *imposing*, and *mirthless*. There is no photo attached. Not even a court sketch like they sometimes show.

After scouring the article a few more times to see if I missed anything, I determine that it simply can't be the same man. My Alexei, even though he's still basically just a stranger, would not commit murder. And he certainly isn't mirthless, even if he is tall and imposing.

I sigh and roll my eyes again at myself. I may make some foolish choices from time to time, just like anyone else, but even I can't be dumb enough to accidentally lose my virginity to a nearly-convicted murderer.

"Nope," I say out loud, shaking my head as though to dispel the accusations buzzing around me like flies. "Just nope."

I set my phone aside and close my eyes, finally allowing myself to just relax and enjoy the bubble bath. I stay in this spot for at least an hour or so, just wallowing and letting my mind wander freely for once. It's not until I am forced to slow down and chill out that I realize just how tired and overworked I am on a regular basis.

I decide to push the whole Alexei versus Dean issue out of my mind for a little while, assuring myself that Alexei is probably just tracking him down to have a stern word with him. Yes. That's it. That's what men around here do, they tell each other to back off.

After my long bath, I get out all pruny and relaxed, and put on the robe. I lazily walk into the kitchen and fix myself a simple sandwich and drink a beer from the fridge. Following Jolene's orders, I sit down in the den and watch dumb cooking shows on TV, eventually falling asleep on the sofa.

The pitter-patter of the rain and the low rumbling of thunder lull me off to slumber, and I have pleasant, vague dreams. It's a long, lazy, much-needed nap, and when I finally wake up, it's to the sound of a big truck crunching over gravel outside. I sit up with a jolt, the memories of the past twenty-four hours dawning on me, and then I go to the window to look outside and see Alexei getting out of the truck. He walks into the house drenched from the rain and smelling of... something foul. He's tracking mud into the house with his heavy boots. I glance at the clock on the wall: it's nearly two-thirty in the afternoon.

Alexei looks at me and I give him a little smile and wave.

"Hi," I say a little meekly.

"Hello," he answers gruffly.

Nervously tucking my hair behind my ears, I suggest, "Maybe you want a shower? Get out of those filthy, wet clothes?"

He nods and gives me a rather forced smile.

"Yes."

Alexei trudges off to the bathroom to shower, leaving me hanging around awkwardly in the den. Suddenly, an urge to investigate possesses me, and I can't banish the thought. While he's in the shower, I quietly slip out the front door and run through the little uncovered patch of yard to the carport. With my heart racing and my hands shaking, I open up the truck on the driver's side, relieved that it's unlocked. I fumble around, my hands feeling out for his wallet in the same place I keep mine. If I could find his ID, I could dispel those nasty thoughts running through my head.

Instead, I feel something else.

My blood runs cold.

Underneath the driver's seat is a warm gun. With trembling, clumsy fingers, I pop the clip out.

There's one bullet missing.

ALEXEI

I pull my boots back on and stand up, seeing myself in the mirror of the dresser in the third outfit I've put on today, none of them too different from each other. A tight white t-shirt hugs my muscles above dark blue jeans, and I pick up a towel to finish drying off my hair.

Usually, putting on a fresh change of clothes is therapeutic for me. It's one of the simple pleasures in life that makes me feel clean and better for it.

But I have a sense of what's about to happen in the near future, either sooner or later. What I have done is not something that I will be able to hide from Daisy for long.

I've covered up murders many times before, of course, sometimes in person, others from a distance. But for some reason, mustering up a lie to tell Daisy feels both wrong and strangely difficult.

I could say I paid him off, gave him that twenty large and he ran off with his tail between his legs. It'd take her a while to believe me, and to feel safe, knowing he's still out there.

But even the thought of not totally soothing all her worries about him leaves me feeling a bit cold. I want her to know he's taken care of *for good* and that he will *never* be able to bother her or hurt her again.

The lie is still safest, though. For me. For her.

When I step out of my room and see the door hanging open, I realize that I might have to face reality sooner rather than later.

Daisy's form darts toward the door from the outside, and then she's inside, slamming the door behind her.

Her strawberry-blonde hair is soaking wet, clinging to her neck and shoulders, and trails of water run down her forehead and past those furious, wild eyes that are full of accusation and fear all at once.

But most of all, her face is contorted with anger. Her teeth are gritted, and her whole body is very slightly shaking. As she looks at me, her face goes even redder with rage, and she strides toward me and looks like she's holding back the urge to try to shove me.

I have a head and shoulders on her, my body rock hard while hers is soft and feminine, but all that anger coiled in her body seems dangerous, even to me.

Instead of shoving me, though, she glares up at me.

And even this way, she looks so beautiful.

There's such purpose in the way she moves, such spirited energy that makes her look so much more alive than anyone I've met in my life. It feels so strange to think these things about someone I've only really known for less than a day, but there's something about Daisy that is simply *different*.

Of course she is.

A few days ago, I never thought I would do such a thing as taking a life without money being exchanged for it. In fact, I hoped I would be able to live out the rest of my life without shedding more blood.

But in my heart of hearts, I knew the whole time that this was a foolish thought.

Killing Dean felt *good*.

She glares up at me for a silent moment that feels like it lasts an eternity before she finally speaks a question that I do not expect.

"Who *are* you?" she hisses, her accent coming out stronger through thick anger.

What a question.

I left my old life behind me hoping to let it rest eternally, and in doing so, I have tried to act like a new person—more like what the young man who left Siberia was like before he took a life might have become.

Nobody can escape their past, though.

"Answer me!" she insists, taking a step closer when I don't respond. I'm still as a statue, reacting to neither her movement nor her tone. "Who the hell are you?"

"Who do you suppose I am?" I say in a quiet, gravelly voice.

"I *thought* you were just some reclusive guy who's running from something he doesn't want to talk about like half the other mysterious strangers out here," she rattles off.

I raise my eyebrows. She's not too far off from the truth.

"Am I not?"

I hear her jaw pop from straining it so much, and she points out the door toward the truck. "I found a gun out there, Alexei."

"Don't you have a gun?" I say mildly. I'm not in too deep. Not yet. I just have to buy some time before I can find a way to make this all better.

"Yes, but-" she shakes her head, frustrated. "You know damn well what I mean! I found a pistol, Alexei. A pistol with a bullet missing, and was that a fucking silencer in there with it?"

"Why were you looking in my truck?" I ask.

"Because..." she stammers, desperately trying to come up with an excuse.

"Because you don't trust me," I finish for her, and she gives me an exasperated look.

"Why is it out there, Alexei?" she asks. "You know damn well how that looks. I need an explanation. What the hell did you go out and do?"

"I told you what I went out to do," I say. Her eyes go wide, and her mouth falls open. "I went to deal with this. And I did."

She reads my face carefully, shock growing on her expression.

"Where is Dean?" she breathes.

"Dean is no longer a problem," I say simply. "You will not see him again, and he won't bother Broken Pine any longer."

Daisy puts a hand to her forehead and paces around the room, going to the window and letting her hand run down to cover her mouth and breathe heavily before she comes back up to me and looks me dead in the eye, trying to hold herself together.

"No more word games," she says. "Alexei, so help me god, I need you to be straight with me and not mince any words."

I do not reply with anything more than a stare, the tension in the air almost deafening both of us.

"Is he dead?" she asks, nearly having trouble forcing the three words out of her mouth.

The directness of the question, her tone... It manages to take even me by surprise. Like everything has just been stripped bare, robbed of pretense and excuses.

I could lie.

It would be the simplest thing in the world. I've had enough time during this conversation to steel my will, even against those endlessly beautiful and searching hazel eyes of Daisy's. It would just be a single word, *no*, and I could tell her that he accepted my offer and left. I would have a few other loose ends to tie up, but that would be the bulk of the work done.

But that would be such a betrayal of Daisy that I'm not sure I could live with myself after the fact. The connection I felt last night with this innocent girl is something new and exhilarating. I am a cold man, I know that, but am I so cold that I can have such a feeling for someone and then turn to deception so soon afterward?

It might not even matter. She could be about to turn me in to the police. Whether or not she does, our relationship might be about to end in its youth.

No matter.

I know what answer I must give.

"Yes."

The single word hangs in the air between us, and I watch all the color drain from Daisy's beautiful, freckled face. Her lip quivers, but she holds her ground and finds the strength for another question.

"Did you...?" she asks, and she doesn't have to

finish the question. I will respect her request to be honest with her.

I nod.

Immediately, her whole body turns, and she tries to run for the front door as she lets out a shuddering gasp.

I catch her by the wrist and tug her back before she can do so much as take a step. I don't grip her so tightly as to hurt her, but my grip is like a rock, and she can't go anywhere.

"Let me go, Alexei," she nearly sobs, keeping her voice to a hoarse whisper. "So help me god, I'll scream and shout so loud the whole town will hear me if you don't let me go."

"He was a monster, Daisy," I say. "You nearly said as much yourself."

"He was a human being, Alexei!" she says, turning to face me with red-rimmed eyes.

"A human the world will be better off without," I insist, taking a step closer to her. Seeing her shrink back is like a knife in my gut, but I can't let her go like this. "He was a sadist, Daisy. He tortured the animals under his care, and he would have treated you just like one if he had gone on living. Look me in the eye and tell me that is not exactly what you've been afraid of since you caught him outside your house."

She doesn't respond. She just glares up at me, a glare full of defiance and disbelief.

"This was for you, Daisy," I say firmly. "I do not kill without purpose, and I've been around the world enough to know a natural-born killer when I see one. Dean was a danger to every vulnerable person and animal in this town. Worse, he knew he could get away with anything he did. How many times have you heard someone say *'boys will be boys'* before turning a blind eye to something he's done?"

She winces, and I know I've struck a truth even she didn't want to confront.

I don't want to tell her point-blank that if I hadn't killed Dean, it would be *her* in a body bag before too long, by his doing. I think she knows it, deep down.

I use my other hand to take her by the small of her back and pull her closer, looming over her and looking into her eyes. She doesn't resist, but she is trembling.

"Daisy, I would not have done this if I didn't fear for your life," I say. "New York City. Moscow. Siberia. You think these places aren't riddled with killers? I know one when I see one."

"It takes one to know one, doesn't it?" she says.

That stings.

We glare at each other for a long moment before I speak again in a slow, deliberate tone.

"Do you think I am like him?" I ask simply.

Her jaw sets, but many moments pass before she replies.

"No," she breathes, letting her head fall a bit. "No, I...I don't think so."

"Men like Dean do not deserve to live," I say emphatically. "They are men who live only for themselves, men who see women as things to take for themselves and hurt them when they fight back. I saw this firsthand. You saw this firsthand. Can you honestly say the world is not a better place without him?"

"I'm no killer," she says weakly.

"No, you're not," I say, and I release her wrist to cup her face in my hands gently. "No blood is on your hands, Daisy. Not a drop. This is on me. This is a path I've walked many times before."

She looks up at me with fear in her eyes again, and I nod.

"I would not have done this if I did not think I could do it quickly, cleanly, and quietly," I say softly. "I know what I'm doing. I'm keeping you safe."

Tears well up in her eyes, large tears of a woman who has been pushed to her limits and has nowhere to turn to. She starts to sob.

I draw her close and press my lips to her quivering ones, and her whole body shudders before I hug her to me. After a moment, she starts to put her hands on my sides.

There is a knock at the door.

She jumps back, eyes as wide as plates, and she looks toward the door in terror.

I don't jump, but my gaze is locked on the door just as intently, my heart pounding.

Shit.

The sheriff.

Sometimes, jobs go quickly and easily. Other times, even if you take every precaution and make all the right moves...something goes wrong in a way you cannot predict. All it takes is for one unnoticed bystander to hear something strange for the police to get involved.

And in a small town like Broken Pine, the reclusive Russian farmer built like a professional fighter and living alone outside town is a prime suspect for just about anything.

"Daisy," I whisper, getting her attention. "I can't control you, nor do I want to. All I can say is please, for both our sakes, don't say anything. Let me handle this."

I don't give her a chance to reply before I cross the living room floor and pull the door open, my mind racing with all my experience telling lies to the authorities.

DAISY

My heart is racing a million miles a minute. I hurriedly wrap the robe more tightly around my body and duck out of the way, pressing myself against the wall as Alexei walks over to answer the door. I watch with wide eyes, breathing heavily as he opens the door slowly and cautiously.

I'm torn, wondering if it would be better or worse for the sheriff to find me holed up in a murderer's house. I know the fingers will already be pointed at me, since Dean told everyone that I was *his* girl. And as far as everyone else knows, he's a good boy who must have been treating me well.

Nobody would ever believe me if I claim that he is—*was*—a menace to society and especially to women. Even though everyone I know seems to like me and respect me, I cannot be certain that they would side with me if it came down to a question of Daisy versus Dean.

The Ashcrofts have been living in Broken Pine for many generations, nearly as long as the Jensons have. The families have lived side by side, bound in friendship and neighborly love for as long as most folks still living can remember. Broken Pine isn't exactly known for its family feuds or, well, conflict in general. There's never anything worth fighting about here, really. At least on the surface.

I strain to hear the first words said, since I can't see who's at the door from this angle.

To my surprise, the voice I hear sounds like it belongs to a child. A little girl's high-pitched, excited squeal of, "Alexei!"

Not half a second later, a tiny girl who could hardly be older than four or five comes barreling through the front door, arms outstretched. She runs straight up to Alexei, throwing her little arms around his leg. She's got gorgeous coppery-red curls pulled into two twin pigtails, flouncing as she hugs Alexei tightly. He chuckles and bends at the waist to pat her on the back as a second voice enters the conversation.

It's a man's voice, but not Alexei's.

"Hey, man. Good to see you!"

Alexei looks up and holds out his hand for the mystery man to shake. They greet each other like old, treasured friends as the little girl clings to Alexei's leg with a huge grin on her freckly face.

"How're you doing?" Alexei asks.

"Great, great. Can't complain. Not that that stops me most of the time," the man jokes in a very familiar country drawl. "Lily here has been keeping me busy, as usual."

"We went camping last weekend!" Lily burst out excitedly.

"We did, that's right," says the man with a good-natured laugh.

"That sounds like a real adventure," Alexei says. "Come on in."

I gasp and panic, wondering if I should bolt across the house and hide in the bathroom or something, not wanting to be caught hanging around this murderer's house in a robe. That might look a little bit compromising.

But before I have a chance to even make that split-second decision, the man and his daughter are walking into the house, and the little girl spots me instantly. Her brown eyes go wide and ecstatic at the sight of me.

"Alexei! There's a lady here!" she gasps, pointing at me with the tactless innocence of a child. Both men look over at me, and as soon as the second man's eyes fall on me, he squints and tilts his head to one side in confusion.

"Hey… Daisy Jenson?" he asks, scratching at his chin thoughtfully.

It hits me that I recognize him, too. It's Bradley Downing, an old classmate of mine from high school. He was a couple grades ahead of me, a senior when I was a sophomore. But I remember seeing him around school.

In a town like Broken Pine, the classes are pretty small, and you get to know everyone quickly enough. I realize, though, that I haven't seen him since high school. Last I heard, he married his high school sweetheart, who happened to be a girl from my grade, Jenny Parsons. She and I were never close friends, but I remember her being a sweet and pretty girl whom everyone got along with. I feel terrible that I never kept up with her and Brad after they were married, but once Daddy died my life kind of got a little crazy.

"Brad," I say, wrapping the robe more tightly around myself and forcing a smile.

"Boy, I never expected to see you here," he chuckles. "How you been?"

"Fine. Just fine," I tell him, feeling extremely awkward standing here in my robe.

"Good to hear! Look, I'm sorry I never got around to your daddy's funeral," he says suddenly, shaking his head. "Lily was just a toddler when it… it happened, and I couldn't find a sitter. It's hard for a single dad, you know. But I do want you to know how sorry I am to have missed it. I should've been there."

"Oh, no. No worries. I'm sure you and Jenny had your hands full," I tell him, smiling, completely missing the *single* dad part.

His face falls instantly. Alexei's jaw tightens and he glances at Brad's face with a concerned look. Brad sighs and ruffles his fingers back through his hair, looking like he's trying to say the right thing.

"What's wrong?" I ask.

"Jenny, uh, well, she died. When Lily was born there were... complications. You know. These things, they just happen sometimes," he explains stiffly.

I feel my cheeks burning.

"Oh my gosh. I'm so sorry, Bradley. I-I didn't know."

"It's okay. We kept it pretty quiet," he says, glancing down at Lily pointedly. Luckily, the little girl seems pretty oblivious to the heavy conversation, as she's currently staring at me with an amused expression.

"Did you say your name was Daisy?" she asks brightly.

I give her a smile and a nod.

"Yes. I'm Daisy."

She grins and jumps up and down, tugging at her father's sleeve.

"Daddy, Daddy! She's a flower, too, just like me!"

All three of us laugh and Brad says, "Yep. That's right. Both flowers."

"I wanna ride Misty!" she says cheerfully, changing the topic completely, as little kids tend to do. Alexei gives one of her pigtails a quick little tug and she giggles, swatting at his hand.

"Alright, let's get you all ready and saddled up, then," he says. "How's that sound?"

"Can I, Daddy?" she asks desperately, peering up at Brad with wide eyes.

He grins and taps her nose with his finger. "Of course, sweetie. Why don't you go on ahead and run out to the stable? Alexei and I will be right behind you."

"Yay!" Lily squeals, jumping up and down in circles with a huge grin on her face. She all but stumbles out the door, taking off in the direction of the stables as quickly as her tiny little legs can carry her.

"Feel free to join us once you're…" Alexei starts off, leaving out the word *decent*.

I blush and nod, waving them on.

"Mhm. Yep. Go on, then. I'll just change real quick."

Brad and Alexei head out, and as soon as the door is closed, I rush to the bedroom to gather up my clothes and put them on in a hurry. My hands are shaking still, and my heart is thumping so hard it feels like I might stop breathing. But I force myself to take a few long, slow breaths, reminding myself that if I'm going to pull this off, I need to act like everything is fine.

I pull on my shoes and my sundress, feeling a little icky to be wearing the same clothes I had on last night, but the only other alternative would be to try and rifle through Alexei's closet and drawers. And I have a strong inkling that he doesn't own a single item of clothing that would come even close to fitting my much tinier frame.

I walk into the bathroom and check out my reflection, wincing a little. Of course, I still have not a single stitch of makeup on, since last night I hopped out of bed and climbed out the window without any plans of interacting with anyone else.

It strikes me suddenly how odd it is that a hand-some guy like Alexei would be interested in a girl like me. I'm not blind or foolish enough to think I'm unattractive, exactly, but I certainly don't consider myself a total knockout. My skin is milky-white, my time in the sun only evidenced by the smattering of freckles across the bridge of my nose and on my shoulders. My hazel eyes are rimmed with pink and there are half-moon shadows underneath them, signs that I haven't been sleeping as much as I should lately, but my lashes are plush and long. My lips are full and soft, my teeth relatively straight and pretty to look at. I reach up and yank my hair out of its messy bun, letting the reddish-gold waves fall softly around my shoulders. I heave a sigh and shrug.

"This is as good as it gets," I say aloud.

I turn on my heel and walk out, opening the front door and heading out into the mid-afternoon sunshine. The dark clouds and rain have all faded away to blue skies and fluffy white clouds. As usual, the prairie weather is completely unpredictable. It occurs to me that Brad and his little girl have probably been waiting all day for the skies to clear so that Lily could ride horses here. I wonder what would have happened if the weather had been nice all day. What if they had showed up here while Alexei was out? How would I have reacted?

I stroll across the open green field toward the stables. The world just seems so calm and peaceful, like it hasn't changed at all. Or maybe gotten a little bit brighter, even.

At the back of my mind floats the pressing event of the day: Dean is dead, and Alexei is the one who killed him. But right now, with the summer sunshine beaming down on my bare skin, the grass dewy with rain underfoot, the smell of wildflowers on the breeze... well, it's easier than one might expect to push that darkness into the forgotten, cobwebby corner of my mind. Right now, I have only the present moment to focus on, and that's exactly what I plan to do.

I approach the stables and the fenced field in

which Lily is perched atop a huge dappled-gray horse. Lily looks utterly enthralled with the experience, her face grinning and bright with joy. Alexei has the horse's lead in his hand as he walks alongside the horse in wide circles. Brad is standing off to the side, his arms crossed over his chest as he watches with a soft, adoring smile.

"Look at me, Daisy!" the little girl calls out as I walk up next to her father.

I smile and wave at her and she erupts into peals of delighted laughter. Brad nudges me with his elbow, beaming.

"She's a handful, that one," he says.

"I can tell," I reply. "But she seems like a great kid. Beautiful, too. That red hair!"

"Yeah," he agrees gently. "She got lucky—looks just like her mama."

"I can definitely see you in there, too, though," I assure him.

He nods slowly.

"Yep. She's got my dimples and, poor thing, she got my stubborn personality, too. But everything else is pure Jenny."

"So, what happened, if you don't mind my asking?" I inquire, keeping my voice low.

He sighs.

"Just one of those things, you know? Jenny got pregnant right after our wedding, and we were so excited. It wasn't planned, of course, but it didn't matter. As soon as we saw Lily's little face on that sonogram machine, we were in love. There was no going back. For the first seven months, everything was perfect. Jenny was in great shape. She had to stop playing softball and everything, naturally, but she was doing her yoga and breathing exercises." He pauses to laugh, then continues, "She even started eating super healthy. Spinach and broccoli and all that, you know. Jenny and I, we'd hit the Saturday farmer's market for all those fresh veggies. She kept tellin' me, 'Brad, I want this baby to be so healthy she makes the Jolly Green Giant jealous.'"

"Yep, sounds like Jenny," I giggle.

"She was always so silly like that," Brad sighs wistfully. "But when it came to her pregnancy, she was so serious. Nothing was going to go wrong, not on her watch. But when the seventh month came... things changed so quickly. Out of nowhere, Jen started getting these awful stomach pains. She was throwing up all the time, having dizzy spells and headaches."

"What was causing it?" I ask curiously.

He shakes his head.

"The doctors weren't sure. None of it seemed life-threatening yet, anyway, so they just brought her in for some testing and sent her back home. But then, on April ninth, around two in the morning, she woke me up screaming in pain. I didn't know what to do, so I rushed her to the hospital over in North

Platte. But even they didn't know what was wrong, so they had her air-lifted all the way to Omaha."

"Oh my goodness," I gasp.

"Yeah. It was horrific. I was so scared, but Jenny — she was so brave. As always. Even as she was drifting in and out of consciousness, she kept sayin' to me, 'It'll all be okay. Don't you worry,'" he says, taking a moment to gather his composure before going on. I pat him on the back and he gives me a quick, appreciative smile.

"Anyway. By the time we got to the big hospital in Omaha, she was barely conscious at all. They had to induce labor. All kinds of fancy complications I don't understand. I'm a country guy, you know. I don't have a clue about that stuff. Lily was born a few hours later, two months early, but otherwise perfectly healthy. Jenny, though— she was in a bad place. They kept her pretty well-medicated until the end, but I knew she was still hurtin'. That was the hardest part. I knew I was gonna lose her, but seein' her in pain was too much."

"God, I'm so sorry, Bradley."

He clears his throat and swipes at his eyes quickly, then gives me a smile.

"I may have lost Jenny, and I miss her every day, but I am so grateful to still have Lily. That little girl has forced me to find strength when I thought I had none left in me. She keeps me going."

"You're a good dad," I tell him honestly. "I can tell.

And my Daddy… Well he raised me all on his own. And I turned out just fine. I'm sure you'll do great with her."

"Thank you. I sure hope so," he says. "And I'm so grateful to Alexei, too. He's been giving Lily horse-back-riding lessons for free. Can you believe that? For free! Even around here, that's unheard of."

"So, do you know him very well?" I ask, trying to be subtle.

Brad gives me a shrug of uncertainty.

"Not very well, no. He's been around town for a couple years, I think. Keeps to himself, mostly. Nothin' wrong with that. Lily and I kind of keep to ourselves, too. I'm so busy with my woodworking business and bein' a single dad, I don't have time to get out much. But as Lily gets older, I'm realizing how badly she needs to be out there in the world, making friends, learning new things. That's why I'm so thankful for these horse riding lessons."

"She seems to really enjoy it," I note.

He chuckles.

"Yeah, she loves it. And she just adores Alexei. I was a little worried she'd be afraid of him, at first. You know, big bulky stranger with a serious face. But nope. She took to him like a fish to water."

"He's good with her, isn't he?" I muse aloud.

"Real good," Brad agrees warmly. "I bet he'd love a kid of his own someday."

I raise an eyebrow at this.

"You think so?"

"Hell yeah," he answers with a laugh. "A good guy like him? He keeps to himself like I do, but at least I've got Lily to keep me company. Alexei, though, I think he probably gets pretty lonely out here on the farm. You know, I bet he wouldn't turn up his nose at the idea of a pretty wife to look after him, either."

He gives me an exaggerated wink and I burst out laughing, rolling my eyes.

"Uh-huh. Point taken," I chuckle. "But to tell you the truth, Alexei and I just met. You know him better than I do already."

"Well, then take it from me: he's one of the good guys. That much I know for sure," Brad tells me with complete sincerity. And as I watch Alexei patiently and gently guiding little Lily on the dappled mare, it's easy enough to believe he's right about that. But still, I can't seem to figure out how to compromise the two different sides of Alexei I have met.

There's Alexei, the stoic, imposing, cold-blooded killer. There's Alexei, the passionate lover who gave me the thrill of my life. And then there's Alexei, the gentle giant who loves kids and treats his fellow man with overwhelming patience and compassion.

How can he possibly be all three at the same time? Which side is the real one?

And how can I figure that out?

By the time the lesson is over and Brad takes Lily back home, the sun is setting on the horizon. The green fields are awash in late afternoon light, the sky turning purplish-gray with streaks of vibrant watermelon-pink. I hang around the stables while Alexei cares for the two horses and the chickens. When he's done, he comes walking slowly over to me where I'm perched on the wooden fence. He has a stony expression on his face, a dark question glowing in his eyes. I know I should ask it. I know I should. A voice in the back of my mind warns me that I shouldn't even be here right now. I shouldn't stick around to see what happens.

If I were smart, I would turn tail and run.

But right now, I don't want words, and I don't want to run away.

I want something else entirely.

As soon as he gets close enough, I wrap my arms around him, pulling him close as I press my lips against his in a passionate, desperate kiss.

ALEXEI

I would be lying if I said the kiss isn't a surprise.

Everything about today has been a careful balancing act of maintaining my emotions and keeping an eye on Daisy's body language. One move on her part could have put me in mortal danger at the drop of a hat, and there would have been no way I could have stopped it without things turning uglier than I'm willing to let them get.

But she maintained her composure the whole time, and now, her warm lips are pressed against mine, full of fire and desire.

I don't question it.

Sometimes, there's no room for that.

My hands go to Daisy's sides, and I lift her up off the wooden fence and draw her closer to me, hugging her tight against my chest as our tongues explore one another. She immediately starts grinding her hips against me, my hand holding her up by the ass and my other hand working its way up the back of her shirt to unhook her bra before I've even started moving.

I walk us back to the door of the house and kick it open. Daisy is completely engrossed in me the entire time, and I'm so into her that I'm amazed I don't let us trip over something and tumble to the ground together.

And even if we had, I don't think that would have stopped us.

We spill into the living room, and I use a leg to slam the door behind me so hard it startles the chickens outside.

Daisy's hands are on my face, holding me to her as she kisses me.

This feels different from last night.

The first time I was with Daisy, we were in the middle of a storm of emotions that she barely had a grip on. She had just escaped a life-threatening situation and thrown herself into a night of drinking, dancing, and tossing all caution to the wind. In the middle of all that, she gave herself to me more than willingly. She was eager to lose her flower, and I was more than willing to take it.

If there was any worry in my mind left over that she regretted it, they're all dispelled now.

I carry her to the wall and slam her against it,

pinning her small, curvy frame between my rock-hard body and the wooden wall behind her. The moment we make impact, she lets out a moan of bliss. My cock is thickening between her legs, which are wrapped around my waist. We push into each other and grind, feeling our sexes getting excited and agitated all at once through the layers of fabric.

We need each other. Right now, in this moment, more than anything else, we crave one another's touch and affection, and we want to spill it into each other.

Last night was good, but this moment feels like plucking the string of an instrument wound so tightly that it's about to snap.

I take control. She tries to move her hands around my body after I pin her to the wall, but I take those hands and push them against the wood, holding her with her arms out and supporting her with my hips. With her exposed, it's the easiest thing in the world for me to ravish the sensitive skin on her neck with kisses and gentle biting. My teeth graze her and nip at her playfully, each time making her twitch and whimper more.

"I need you in me," she whimpers desperately. "Alexei, I've never needed anything more. Please."

"You'll get it when I give it to you," I growl. My hot breath tickles the ear I bring my mouth close to, and a shiver runs up her whole body.

I let her arms go and take her hips in my hands,

using them to help me grind against her pussy better. I feel her getting hotter through the denim, and the look she gives me with those shimmering eyes is fuller of desire than I've seen in her yet.

"I've awakened something in you, Daisy," I say in a low tone, thick with need. "For better or worse, there's something in you that has been released and cannot be put back."

"Good," she says without a moment's hesitation. "I want it that way."

"You have no idea what to do with it, *kotyonok*," I whisper. I bring a hand to her chin and take hold of it, forcing her to look into my eyes while I play with her lower lip with my thumb. "You're new to this. I will guide you."

"You can do anything you want with me," she breathes. "I just need you so fucking bad, Alexei."

"Do you?" I chuckle, and I tug at the loose bra on her, helping her wiggle out of it before I slip my hand under her dress and start fondling her breasts.

The weight of her whole body in my arms is exquisite. The feeling of her pressed against me makes my heart race, and when I feel her nipples stiffening at my touch, it electrifies me. "You have no idea what you want," I growl, "no idea what you're asking for from me."

"I want to find out," she gasps, and I pinch her nipple.

She squeals and wiggles in my grasp, but I have

such a grip on her that she can't get away. She has to endure me as I flick and pinch her stiff tits and grope her smooth, firm breasts. My body is as hard as the face of a cliff, and it holds her exactly the ways I want it.

I turn and carry her over toward the couch in slow, deliberate steps, still toying with her full breasts as I go. I toss her onto the soft cushions and watch her bounce and turn to face me, her blushing face excitedly watching me for whatever I do next.

Looming over her, I stoop down to pull off her shoes, then take hold of her panties and yank them down, exposing her to me roughly and viciously. The sight of her exposed lower lips is tempting, but I stay focused and pull her slip up over her head, leaving her utterly naked before me while I glower down at her body, still fully clothed myself.

"You want to learn?" I growl, kneeling and stroking some of that beautiful strawberry blonde hair. "You need to know your own body. How do you touch yourself?"

She bites her lip and looks at me with a worried expression, not sure how to respond, and I realize what she's conveying.

"You...don't?"

"I was always taught it isn't right," she whispers. "That it wasn't natural. Something you did if you couldn't control yourself."

"Can you control yourself right now?" I ask with a broadening, wicked grin.

She breathes a quick, shallow breath and shakes her freckled head, and I feel my cock so stiff it could burst from my pants.

"I…" She swallows. "I used to use a pillow. I'd hug it tight and use my hips until…" She blushes.

I lean in and kiss her on the lips, savoring the moan she gives me in response.

"There's nothing wrong with it," I say. "Only that you've been missing out on so many better ways."

I hold up two fingers to her, which she watches with fascination. "Do this."

She imitates me, holding up two of her fingers together. I take her hand and slip those fingers into my mouth, letting my tongue roll up and down them until they're wet and glistening before I take them out.

I guide her hand down to her pussy, and I place those wet fingertips on her clit and gently push in.

She gasps and goes a darker shade of red, and I run a hand over her thigh, squeezing the sensitive skin possessively.

"Small circles," I instruct her in a commanding tone. She blinks those big, innocent eyes at me, then looks down at her pussy and slowly traces a circle with her fingers.

As she does, she shudders and whimpers, but her eyes go even wider at the sensation.

"Good," I growl, "but look at me."

She obeys, turning her pretty head up to me as I stand up. "Don't stop," I tell her when I notice her slowing down, and she bobs her head hurriedly and keeps going, clumsily finding her favorite pace and making little circles on that swollen, sensitive nub.

I kick my shoes off and push them aside as I stand to my full height, my big chest taking long, deep breaths as I drink in her form. Naked, innocent, ready to be plucked, touching herself on my couch. This girl is all mine, and I'm going to make sure she loves every second of it.

I bring my strong hands to the hem of my shirt and slowly pull it up over my head, revealing each defined muscle one by one as the white fabric slides off. When it's off, I toss it aside and waste no time giving the leather belt around my waist the same treatment. My abs form a V that plunges toward my crotch, and the leather grazes the edge of it while it comes off my body and clatters to the floor.

While I strip, revealing more of my statuesque body bit by bit, Daisy gets excited. Her cheeks stay a steady deep pink, and I can't help but remember that this is the deepest into sin this young woman has ever been.

I am a corruptor, I realize. This woman was perfectly innocent and preparing herself for a chaste life before marriage to a country husband, all before I came along and claimed her.

If that is the price we must pay for our little games, I will pay it gladly, and she seems to be of the same mind.

She starts moving her fingers in smaller, faster circles, biting her lip and watching me. One of her hands grips the couch cushion, but I shake my head at her.

"Your nipples. Touch them. Play with them like I did."

"Yes, sir," she says in a hushed tone, and she brings a nearly-shaking hand to her breast and starts fondling it. That draws a gasp of air from her, and she shuts her eyes, chewing on her lip.

"Eyes on me," I growl, and she obeys, bobbing her head apologetically. I crack a smile. "Good girl."

"Oh god," she groans in desire, "I love it when you call me that."

"You have to earn it," I say in a husk, and with that, I unbutton my pants, one button after the other. Before long, the thick trunk of my shaft is visible as I start to slide the denim down.

She starts to push her hips up in a rhythm with her hand motions, and I nod approvingly. "You're getting better."

I bring my pants down and shake them off, and I reward her with the sight of my fully-erect, bulging cock. She hasn't yet seen it like this, proudly on display from a distance, along with the rest of my form. My legs are impeccably cut, and every muscle in my tight calves is chiseled to perfection.

I am not modest about my body. I am a trained killing machine. My body and instincts are my livelihood—or they were, supposedly, but my idea of retirement seems to be falling apart all around me. But if that means keeping Daisy at my side, then it might not be so bad after all.

I grab a chair and drag it to face Daisy a foot from the couch, and I take a seat in it, letting my cock stick straight up. She looks at my massive shaft, gazing at the vein-ribbed girth bobbing up in the air, pulsing and twitching at the sight of her touching herself.

"You're slowing down," I chide her gently, and she whimpers, picking up the pace again and driving herself further to orgasm. "I want you to make yourself come. Can you do that for me, *kotyonok*?"

"What does that word mean?" she gasps as she touches herself, her thighs squirming desperately.

"Kitten," I reply with a wicked smile, and she whimpers desperately.

I wrap my big hand around my shaft, and I slowly bring it up and down its length, warming my whole girth.

She pants as I start to work my thick manhood, but my eyes are glaring right at her, paralyzing her. She starts to close her thighs to massage herself, but I shake my head.

"Legs open. I want to watch you."

"Yes, sir," she whimpers in response, and I'm proud to train her so well.

"Faster," I order her. I start massaging my cock a little faster to encourage her, and I draw my thumb around the dark crown at the top before letting my palm slide to the base, pushing against my balls ever so slightly, then back up. I start pumping my shaft faster and faster, gaze not moving from Daisy.

"You did this," I say in a thick husk. "Last night, this is the beast that you tamed. This is what I had sunk deep inside you, deflowering you. Do you want this again?"

"God, yes," she whimpers, a pout to her tone that makes my cock twitch and pulse in my hand. She seems to realize the effect that has on me, and she opens her soft lips to speak more. "I need to feel you inside me, Alexei. I want you to fill me up again. It felt so fucking good last time. Was it good for you?"

"You have no idea," I growl, letting my head tilt forward as I work my shaft, and a bead of precum beads up at the tip of my cock, spilling out of my slit and wetting the dark crown. She watches it as if it's precious gold spilling, twitching almost as if she wants to come and take it before it's gone.

"Don't stop," I order her, glaring at her with that piercing gaze, my whole body responding to her without even touching her. Her beauty is such that it's all I need to get me going.

"I'm so close," she whimpers. "I-I'm just nervous!"

"I'll give you so much more soon," I growl. "Come on, good girl, just a little further…"

That spills her over the edge. Her mouth falls open, and she lets out a gasp as her face goes bright red. She tries to snap her thigh shut as the sensation overwhelms her, but I stand up and stride forward immediately, prying her legs apart and forcing her to see it through. Her hand starts shaking, but I put my hand over it and use it to keep massaging her clit all the way through the orgasm as she thrashes and squirms on the couch, orgasmic gasps escaping her lips.

Finally, the orgasm comes to an end, and I take my hand off hers, watching her pant and crack her eyes open to look up at me.

I must look terrifying. My body looms over her entirely, and my cock is stiff, pointed right at her wet pussy.

"Things are better when you listen to me," I growl thickly. "I won't steer you wrong."

"I want to listen to you no matter how you steer me," she says, sounding almost ashamed of herself. "I'd listen to you whether I want to or not. I need you so bad right now, Alexei."

I grip her thighs and put a knee on the couch, drinking in the scent of her in the air.

"I'm going to take you bare again," I say, each syllable heavy and meaningful. "Do you want that?'

She softly nods her head, and with that, I put my cock's tip to her pussy. It comes alive at the familiar feeling, so soft and wet, so ready for me, so tight.

I put my hands around her waist, and without a second thought, I enter her.

She drinks in a deep gasp and closes her eyes for just a moment, biting her lip, then looks up at me with lidded eyes and a dreamy face, reaching up to put a hand to my cheek when I feel that my cock is as deep inside her as it will go.

Then, she asks me the last question I expected to hear.

"Alexei...what did it feel like to kill a man?"

DAISY

I gaze up into Alexei's eyes, my breath caught and held in my throat as my heart pounds rapidly. I wonder if he can feel it. Feel the wild drumbeat in my ribcage, that unrelenting rhythm kicked up several notches by his mere presence, by his hot breath on my skin, his hard body pinning me down.

I feel like I'm being torn in two totally different directions.

On the one hand, I should be fearful. I know I should be. Hell, I should be trying to fight him off. I should be squirming out of his grasp and making a dash for the door. By now, my feet ought to be carrying me out of this farmhouse, lifting me over the emerald-green fields and through the tall trees of the forest brimming the property. If I were smart, there would be a puff of Daisy-shaped smoke where my body is. Alexei would be grasping at nothing but air while I ran for the hills, screaming my head off for someone to come save me.

That's one side of my mind right now. The other side tells a completely opposite story.

That side of me wants to stay right where I am. No, it's worse than that. This crazy, wild side is just now being born. I never had a wild side before I met Alexei. That's how I ended up with a guy like Dean Ashcroft in the first place. He seemed like the safe choice. The smart choice. The one my father would have picked out for me if he were still alive to do so. The kind of man everyone expects me to end up marrying.

I did everything right.

I followed the rules.

And I never got the pay-off everybody promised me. Be a good girl and good things will come to you. But you know what? They lied. They were wrong. I did what I was told and I still got burned. I ended up in a tangled mess with a sociopathic farm boy who wanted to cow me into subservience and make me the kind of timid domestic servant guys like him want in a wife. So I'm finished with that, with following the rules. It's time to toss aside my inno-cence and my good-girl image and embrace the darkness.

Alexei is my darkness. I know that if I stay with him, if I continue to give myself up to him entirely, the dark will consume me. Envelop me like a warm shadow, changing me, molding me, sculpting me into a brand new version of myself. A version those who know me probably won't recognize. But that's a good thing. Because I'm tired of who I used to be, who I have always been. I need something more, and I just know Alexei can give it to me.

But if I'm going to jump off this cliff with him, I can't shy away from the fear, from the shadows. He has a shadowy past, and there's blood on his hands—and not just for the first time. He's done this before, and I know it. But I need to know more. I have to ask the scary questions, and I have to accept whatever terrifying answer he can offer me.

"What did you say?" he growls, sending little vibrations down through my body.

I narrow my eyes at him and repeat the question in a low, soft voice. "Tell me what it feels like to kill a man. I want the details, Alexei. I want to know how it felt to listen to his heart stop beating, to have blood on your hands, to feel someone's blood run cold."

His heart pounds against his chest, and his hips thrust, as if to distract me. It works for just a moment before I look up at him with lusty, pleading eyes.

"You shouldn't ask questions you don't want the answers to," he grunts, leaning down to kiss me and shut me up. But I dig my fingernails into the hard muscles of his back and take his lower lip into my mouth, biting down hard. He doesn't yelp in pain or pull away. He merely groans with mingled annoyance and arousal, like he can't quite decide if he's angry at me or just even more turned on.

I hope it's both. I want to rile him up. I want to see that dark side of him rear its ugly head. I need him to show me his scars.

He breaks away, but only barely. He pauses to delicately brush a loose lock of my hair out of my face and tuck it gently behind my ear as he looks into my face. His eyes drink in every curve and angle of my face, following the lines of my cheekbones, my jaw, the cupid's bow of my lips. But he doesn't meet my gaze. Not yet. It's like he's sizing me up.

I wonder desperately what he sees when he looks at me.

"I mean it," I whisper back fiercely. "Tell me the truth. I won't accept lies from anyone anymore. Not again."

"I have not told you a single lie about myself yet," Alexei retorts, finally meeting my eyes. The blaze in his stare sends shivers down my spine but I won't back down.

"Not telling the whole story is a lie's next-door neighbor," I reply, parroting a line my father used to tell me when I was a child. It feels weird to be talking to him at such an intimate moment, but it also feels *right*. Like we can't hide from each other now.

The flicker of a faint smile crosses Alexei's lips and fades away as quickly as it came. He cups my cheek in his huge hand, and I can feel the callouses there. I wonder how he got these callouses. From farm work? It's possible. But I know there are other rough, ugly parts of him that he keeps hidden from the world, and those are the parts I most desperately want to see.

"You are too wise and foolish at the same time," he tells me, shaking his head.

I tighten my legs around his waist, clenching my pussy to tighten around his cock. His lips fall open in an appreciative groan, which turns me on beyond belief. I like this little modicum of control I can wield over him. Over this powerful man who could break me and toss me aside without a second thought. That kind of power, I am quickly realizing, is intoxicating. Completely and utterly corrupting. But I want it, more than anything.

"I'm done being cautious," I whisper, frowning at him. "Caution has rarely served me very well in the past. I won't live that way anymore. Tell me the *truth*."

"Killing feels like nothing you've ever felt before," he answers, albeit reluctantly. His voice is so low and rasping it could almost be a hiss. He leans in to speak right against the shell of my ear, which makes me

149

tremble. Goosebumps pop up on my skin as I hold my breath again, listening to his every word. "It is exhilarating to be so in control."

"So," I manage to gasp, "You enjoy it?"

He grazes his teeth along the soft flesh of my neck, making my eyelids flutter and a moan roll out of my throat. "No. There is no joy in taking a life, Daisy."

"Then why do you do it?" I ask, rolling my hips to slide his cock in and out of me.

"Why do you think?" he snarls. He slides a hand underneath my head to cradle me like I'm some delicate, fragile piece of china he's afraid to shatter.

I shake my head ever so slightly, still staring up at him wide-eyed and open-mouthed.

"I-I don't know," I confess.

He dives in to kiss me deeply, his tongue probing into my mouth. He rocks his hips, pulling almost all the way out of me before spearing back into me hard. I whimper in glorious pain and pleasure.

"Good. Let's keep it that way," he hisses between gritted teeth. My eyes roll back in my head as he fucks me harder, slipping in and out faster and faster, striking that deliciously sensitive spot deep inside my aching cunny.

"Oh my goodness," I whine, my breaths coming ragged and quick now as he fucks me closer and closer to the brink. But this time I don't want him to ravish me while I just lie limp and useless in his arms. I want to give him everything he's giving me. I want this to be an equal affair, two-sided and passionate. I cling to him as hard as I can, my heels digging into his bare ass while his cock pumps into me. I'm moaning and clenching, my whole body shaking as he rocks back and forth.

"Is it— is it about control?" I gasp.

"What do you think?" Alexei growls back.

As he pushes deeper inside me I cry out and pierce the skin of his back with my nails, choking and moaning with bliss. "I wish— I wish I could be in control," I whimper. "Just once."

"Are you sure that's what you want?" he asks, kissing my neck and burying his face in my hair as he pummels my pussy with his massive cock. It feels like he could tear me apart, split me right down the middle. And the terrible thing is, I would let him. Eagerly. I would welcome my own destruction as long as he's the one destroying me.

"I don't know," I murmur. "I don't know anything anymore."

"Sometimes, the less you know, the better," he answers roughly.

"I'm tired of feeling so helpless, Alexei," I tell him honestly. "I want to feel like I have some say in my own life. It just moves so fast…"

He grabs me and in one swift, smooth movement he flips us around so that he's lying on the couch on his back, with me straddling him on top. From this angle, his cock is buried so deep inside me that I can feel the ache in my abdomen. The sudden shift of fullness inside me makes me momentarily speechless, my eyes rolling back as a spell of dizziness washes over my body. When the dizziness subsides, I open my eyes wide and peer down at him. His hands are gripping my hips tightly, a fire burning brightly in those intense eyes.

"You want control?" he says in a gruff voice. "Take it."

I bite my lip, blushing, unsure of how to proceed. This is what I asked for, I think, but I'm new to this. "Show me," I whisper plaintively.

A wry, fiendish smile crosses his handsome face. He lifts his hips, rolling them as he holds onto me, moving me up and down on his cock. I gasp with pleasure and catch on instantly, leaning forward to steady myself on his chest while I ride him, slowly at first, then faster. With every roll of my hips, his cock stiffens inside me, spearing at that secret place that sends me trembling and moaning every time.

I brace my legs on either side of him, bouncing up and down on his shaft, then rocking back and forth, feeling that delicious friction between the base of his cock and my over-sensitized clit. Alexei sits up slightly, leaning on his elbows so I can lean forward and kiss him while I bounce on his cock. I breathe raggedly, whimpering and moaning with every stroke.

"Feels good, doesn't it? To take control of your own pleasure," he growls.

"Oh my—oh my god," I breathe. "Yes, yes, yes."

"Go as slow or as fast as you want. Hard or soft. Tell me what you need," he commands. "Don't be afraid of your own desires, Daisy. Don't wait. Don't worry. Just take what you want when you want it. I can handle whatever you ask of me."

"Harder," I gasp. "Faster."

Alexei sits up and pulls my legs around his waist, now bucking his hips in tandem with mine to intensify the depth and power of every single stroke. I'm crying out, tossing my head back while he fucks me. He leans forward to kiss my forehead, my cheeks, my neck. His hands slide up to cup my breasts, rolling my nipples between his fingers.

Tendrils of electric pleasure shoot down through my body, circling around my pulsating cunny. He's pounding into me now harder than before, sweat beading and pooling down my spine and his as we meet every stroke with a gasping sigh, the both of us ratcheting higher and higher, closer to the edge.

"Reach down deep inside yourself, my angel," he snarls. "Reach in and tell me your darkest needs, your purest desires. Give them breath. Make them real."

I do as I'm told, my mind screaming at me the answer.

"I want you— I want you to fill me up," I whisper roughly.

"Yes, tell me everything," he prompts me.

"I want you to come inside me, Alexei. I want you to make me yours. I don't want to be careful. I don't want to be safe. I want danger, I want risk, I want— oh god," I mewl, shuddering as my body is wracked with a powerful orgasm. I can feel my pussy clenching and unclenching tightly, and Alexei doesn't let up for even a second.

"So good," he hisses, "so very good. Come for me, Daisy."

"I want *you* to come. Give it to me," I snarl, surprised at how insistent I sound. How desperate and debauched. Who have I become?

And why am I happier to be this new version of myself? Shouldn't I be afraid? Or ashamed?

But I'm not.

I feel nothing but utter freedom, total release. And it's addictive. I need more. Always more. I know I should be careful. Alexei could knock me up. I could end up like Jenny Parsons. But I don't care. In fact, the idea that this powerful, virile man could pump me full of his come and make me pregnant only turns me on more.

The danger, the risk…

I want to embrace it all with no fear. Dean is gone. Dead. No longer a threat to my life, to my happiness. I'll be damned before I let another living soul take my freedom away like that. Never again will I worry like I used to. From now on, I will live for pleasure and excitement and nothing else. And I know that if I just stick with Alexei, life will abide. Pleasure will take over where pain used to dwell, and my days will be sweet and heavenly like in my dreams.

Funny how it takes being bad to make things good. I have to embrace the darkness to find heaven on earth.

"Ask me again," he commands. I can feel his thrusts becoming more erratic, and I pick up the pace to match him, unwilling to be outpaced.

"Do it," I beg, "Come inside me, Alexei. Fill me up. Please. Now."

With a few short pumps, he kisses me hard, his huge hands gripping my ass, and I can feel it—his cock bursting inside of me, his hot, sticky seed filling up my tight little hole. I clench around him, eking out every last precious drop, not wanting a single bit of him to go to waste.

He holds me for a minute, the two of us just heaving and gasping, drinking in each other's warmth. Our scents mingle together in the still air, his cock slowly, slowly stilling inside of me. I wish we could stay like this forever, but eventually, Alexei gives me one last kiss and lifts me away from him. He stands up, offering me his hand without a word.

As I take it and stand beside him, I feel a rush of

dizziness. And then the slick sensation of his seed leaking down my thighs. I smile to myself, reveling in how filthy, how delicious it all is, letting myself be dirty and dangerous with this remarkable man. He leads me by the hand down the hallway to the bathroom, turning on the shower so we can get cleaned up. As we step inside, he presses me to his chest, letting the hot water rush down over our aching bodies. For a few moments, we are silent, just letting the moment be soft and peaceful. But before long, my curiosity, that unrelenting voice in my head, urges me to speak my mind.

Almost as though he can read my thoughts, Alexei says gently, "Ask it."

I look up at him, at the steam rising around us and the water streaming down his sharp cheekbones, and I ask the question lingering in my mind. "In New York... did you escape a murder conviction? I have to know. Was that you, Alexei? Is it true?"

ALEXEI

I knew the question was on her lips before she even started to ask it, and for once, I hate being right.

Our eyes lock for a long time. Both of us are searching one another's souls for answers to different questions. She's still so innocent, so naive that it almost makes me feel guilty just for letting these questions cross her mind. She expects me to lie to her, just like she expected me to lie to her about killing Dean. She wants me to be a liar as well as a murderer, I realize.

That would make things so much simpler for her. She would be able to live with herself for leaving me.

And I would let her go, if she wished it.

But I cannot give her the answer she wants. I can only give her the truth.

Because while she searches my eyes for that

answer, I search hers to know whether she can stand to share a bed with me when she knows the kinds of things I have done throughout my life. It took me long enough to be able to live with myself. I became cold to my ferocity, my brutal efficiency.

I sleep soundly. Will she be able to?

I answer.

"Yes."

She looks at me long and hard before I take the next words from her lips.

"You knew. You knew before the question was even finished leaving those beautiful lips of yours. Why did you ask?"

"I had to know if you would lie to me," she replies quietly.

"You have your answer," I say. "What will you do with it?"

She's quiet for a long time, unmoving. As I gaze into her face, I watch the flecks of water on her forehead build up until they're too heavy, and they run down her face in thin streams, down like little tributaries to join the rivers of water pouring out her hair, down her breasts, between her thighs, and down her knees to the drain. She isn't moving, but nothing about her is still, ever.

"Tell me why," she says at last, her voice thick. "Who was he, Alexei?"

"His name," I start, "was Earl McPherson. When he turned eighteen, he joined up with the Irish mafia in Brooklyn and started running rackets like his bosses told him. He liked the money. The fear and respect made him bold. Violent. Willing to kill. His first blood was an old man who couldn't pay back the loans he took out for his wife's medical bills. He became hired muscle, and soon, he had another dozen rival gang members as notches on his belt. He was strong, and he knew he could get away with much. Too much. At a party, he met the daughter of one of my bosses. He wanted her. She refused him. He killed her."

Daisy looks stunned. I watch the last shards of innocence leave her eyes as she takes in the story behind that particular hit, realizing it's all true. I go on.

"Of course, we could not abide this, but he was too influential for his own people to deal with him. My then-superiors paid me $200,000 to end his miserable life. I did it."

Daisy's mouth is hanging open. I come closer to her, and she takes a step back. I put one hand on the cool glass wall of the shower, then the other, pinning her between my arms as I look down at her, bringing my face close to hers. We're so close that the water splashing off her face hits me.

"Earl McPherson was not the first. And he was not different from any other of them."

"Alexei..." she breathes, "how many have you killed?"

ALEXIS ABBOTT

"I am a hitman, Daisy," I say, slowly and clearly. "And I am one of the best. What you saw in the newspaper was the one time I had a kink in my plans. The one stain on my perfect track record."

"Is that all it is to you?" she croaks.

"Yes," I say coldly. "Because those men, Daisy? Every single one of them was scum. McPherson wasn't even the worst man I killed. I am the best, and because of that, I get to choose what contracts I take. I do my research. Every man I kill, I know his life in the most minute details, down to when he took his first jobs and who his bosses were. I kill rapists. Murderers. Sex traffickers. Pimps. I want to tell you something that I learned my first year doing this, Daisy. Those men's lives are worth more as the money that built this fucking farm than as the horrible ways they carried on as scum of the earth."

I have never spoken to anyone about this before.

Daisy has not budged an inch since her first step back, and she looks up at me with eyes that do not waver. I still don't know what it is about this girl that makes me able to open up, and I don't know what she will do now that I have.

"Doesn't that make you a murderer too, Alexei?" she says, barely above a whisper.

I look hard at her for a long time, then nod slowly.

"The men I killed were the kind the law could never pin down. They made the world a worse place, profited off it, and walked away without a single consequence. If you want to call it that, then yes, I became a murderer so I could cleanse the world of that. I am not like them. And I left that life behind me. I am not a killer any longer."

As she looks at me more, I realize she has found her courage, and she speaks again, this time with more purpose.

"Not anymore? Then what about Dean?"

Damn her.

I lower my arms and step back so that the water runs over my face, and I run my hands over it, feeling the heat through my hair washing away my sins.

"Dean was an exception," I say. "A one-time exception."

"How do I know that?" she asks. "How do I know you're not just lying to me? How do I know you aren't still killing people based out of this one-stop-light town where nobody would come looking for you?"

I look down at her, and I smile. That's not a bad idea. She has good instincts.

Wrapping my hand around the back of her head, lacing my fingers into her soaking-wet hair, I draw us into a kiss. When it finally breaks, I bring my lips to her ear.

"Because I did it for you, Daisy."

I step out of the shower, leaving her standing

there while I grab a towel and dry myself off. I head into the bedroom while the water is still running, and I wrap the towel around my waist as I go to the kitchen to get a drink.

This girl asks many questions.

The ice clinks into the glass, followed by the smooth, clear vodka I pour over it, and I swirl it around a few times before I hear the sound of bare feet padding down the hallway and pausing in the entrance to the kitchen.

I take a drink, then turn to face Daisy, who's standing there in my oversized bathrobe, wet hair dripping behind her, eyes glaring at me. I raise an eyebrow, then hold up the bottle of vodka, offering her some. She starts to look indignant and shake her head, but finally, she frowns and nods.

"How did you get involved in… all this?" she asks.

I raise an eyebrow, and she swallows.

"You know what I mean," she clarifies.

I pour her a glass of vodka and mix it with some of the orange juice in the fridge, then hand her the glass before making my way to the counter and sitting down and thinking for a few long moments. I haven't been asked to recount how I came to this life in a very long time. I hoped I never would.

I always imagined the day I'd be called to answer for my life of crime would be the day I stood trial before a court of law. That, or I'd be long dead before anyone picked up on my trail.

Never did I think I'd be talking about it with a country girl who's more than a head shorter than me.

I look long and hard at her while she sips the screwdriver and makes a face at how strong I made it, and it makes me chuckle before I speak.

"You know, I've never told anyone the things I've said so far, much less what you're asking."

"And why do you think that is?" she asks.

"If you knew me," I say, "you'd have your answer."

"Has there been anyone you'd want to open up to?" she asks cautiously.

"No," I say. I look down at my drink for a moment, then take another swig before I speak more. "My life has been a solitary one. This was partly my choice. I was young when I joined."

"Joined?"

I look her dead in the eye, then bring a finger up to the large red and black star emblazoned on my chest. "The Bratva," I say.

"Br...?" she repeats, trailing off with a look of confusion on her face as she steps further into the kitchen and takes a seat on the table.

"Bratva," I say again, more slowly this time. "It is a Russian word. It means simply *brotherhood* in Russian. But it is much more than that. It is several groups of Russian men across the world who carry out business. We're organized. Principled...in theory."

"A mafia," she breathes, and I see some color drain from her face before she takes a longer drink of her stiff screwdriver.

"The police would call it that, yes," I say, and I smile at the sight of her eyes going wider. "In theory, we look out for each other. We're comrades. But the reality is a somewhat different situation. It was all politics. But as for me, my talents had me rising through the ranks somewhat independently."

"You were doing this from the very start?"

"Almost. Sooner than most," I admit, giving it a little thought myself. "Usually, they have young recruits like me doing things like guard duty, sometimes going to our rivals and causing trouble in a group. But I tended to attract unwanted attention that way, both from our enemies as well as other ambitious young men in our ranks." I crack a smile. "I made them look bad. So, the bosses decided I was more valuable working in the shadows."

She's quiet for a long time, looking into her drink, probably wishing it was kicking in faster. She takes another drink, draining a third of the glass and swallowing with eyes shut tight. She shakes her head at the bite.

"Careful, don't make yourself sick," I say mildly.

"I just...I never knew all this was real," she says. My eyebrows go up.

"Not real?"

"I mean, you see it on TV, but you've seen what

Broken Pine is like. The most exciting thing that happened in the past five years was the time one of my neighbors' goats accidentally got into the seat of a tractor and got it moving. There's nothing like *you* here, no mafia, no-"

"No killers?" I ask, stepping forward after draining my glass and setting it aside. "No violent men who'd hurt people? Really, Daisy?"

She seems to shrink in my shadow, but she gets my meaning, and she nods. "I guess it's easy to ignore things like that when you're not looking hard enough."

"That's what all of New York City does every day," I say. "Contract killers, enforcers, it's all right there under their noses, but only a few people know it's there, and fewer actually look on that under-world with their own eyes. Me, I thrived in it. I started by picking off lowlife loan sharks who ruined other people's lives. Then it was pimps who overstepped their boundaries. Before long, I was settling scores between rival gangs. I was always quick, quiet, and efficient. Nothing is in more demand in a man like me than those qualities."

She's staring out the window now, and her face is unreadable. I wonder whether her mind is wondering about running off during the night, or trying to call the police while I sleep.

"Why here, though?" she asks at last. "Why Broken Pine?"

I chuckle. "Wish I'd come to some other hapless small town?"

"No, I don't mean that," she says. "I just...I don't know, I'm just trying to understand all this."

"The short answer is, exactly the reasons you like this place," I say, crossing my arms matter-of-factly. "New York became a hotbed of politics the higher I climbed. When enough powerful people fear that you could kill them, they become a lot more interested in what you do."

"You were *too* good at your job," she says, cracking a faint smile of her own.

"Something like that," I say, laughing. "Too many dinners, too many cloak-and-dagger meetings in dark places, too many enemies smiling like friends with open arms and a knife in each hand to stab me in the back. The more valuable you are, the more dangerous you are. But they came to rely on me. I was a tool that many people wanted, and soon, I was under pressure to do jobs that I refused. You can only refuse powerful people so long before assassins of your own start coming after you. So, I retired."

It is an abrupt end to probably the most I've ever spoken at once at a time, and Daisy looks almost dazed trying to take it all in. I've just radically changed how she sees the world, and I feel a pang of guilt because of it. But if she wants to be with me, she needs to know all this. Even if it makes her leave.

Maybe it's better that way, for her.

"Now, I have a question for you," I say, and she looks up at me as I close the distance between us and put my hands on her shoulders. "Why do you act so skeptical of my methods...when you yourself asked me what it feels like to kill?"

Her eyes shine up at me, and she chews her lip a little before she puts together an answer.

"I...I guess I wanted to know what makes you able to do it so well. How you do that with a clean conscience."

I think about that for a few moments before I speak again.

"Control," I say slowly. "It's something I never had growing up. Control over my destiny. Over whether good or bad people have a say in my life, in the world. That control means everything to me—a man who's been across the world, mostly not by his own choice."

She looks at me for a long time before she nods, understanding.

"Can you show me that control?" she asks in an almost guilty whisper.

I raise an eyebrow in question, and she speaks again.

"Can you show me how to shoot a gun?"

DAISY

*I*t's barely the break of dawn when Alexei gently nudges me awake. My eyelids flutter open and I smile into his handsome face. The first few streams of pale morning light are shining in through the window of his bedroom, illuminating the sharp angles of his cheekbones. The fire in his eyes isn't put out yet, but it's more of a flicker than a blaze at the moment. He looks at me with all the care and concern of a guardian angel. I wonder if he's been watching me as I sleep. Oddly enough, the thought of him doing that doesn't upset me. If it was anyone else, I might find it creepy or even scary. But something about having Alexei look over me while I'm vulnerable and unsuspecting just makes me feel safer than before.

Like he's ready to kill for me.

He's done it once already.

That realization washes over me again, but this time it feels softer. Warmer. Less like an electrical jolt and more like a splash of tepid water to the face. Waking me up. Reminding me that right now, and all night, I have been lying in the den of the beast, but I'm not his prey. I'm his ward. I'm the one he will fight for, tooth and nail and shining bullet.

Alexei has already proven himself to me, and he continues to do the same again and again, regarding me with the same awe and delicate touch one might show to a treasured relic or precious heirloom. Or a prized orchid. I'm breakable and valuable in his eyes. I don't quite know what it is about me that drew him so close, but I'm glad to have him here with me. I'm relieved to have him on my side, because lord knows I could never survive being his enemy. Although something tells me there aren't a lot of women on his bad side. He treats me so well that I can't imagine him ever mistreating another woman.

He goes after the bad men, like Dean. That's what he told me and that is what I choose to believe. It's better this way, at least for now. I have done my digging, and now it's time to wait and see.

"You're beautiful when you sleep," Alexei says softly. He raises a hand to lightly trace the shape of my lips with his finger, gazing at me with such intense attention that it almost makes me blush. I am not used to being looked at this way. Sure, men have often stared at me or rather, gawked at me, more appropriately. I have had men look me up and down, give me that filthy, appraising once-over. Dean stared at me like I was an unruly child he was trying to set straight. But Alexei watches me in a different way, even if I can't one-hundred-percent put my finger on what that difference is.

"What time is it?" I ask, my throat scratchy from sleep. I look around for a clock. Alexei strokes my hair, not looking away for a moment.

"Just after six," he answers. "Maybe I should let you sleep longer. I'm sorry."

"Don't apologize," I tell him. A slow smile spreads across my face. I sit up and place my hand over his on my cheek, leaning into it warmly. "Waking up to see your face is never a bad thing, I can promise you that."

"I hope I didn't frighten you last night," he says, moving closer.

I shake my head, still smiling. I turn to gently kiss the palm of his hand, closing my eyes and letting my eyelashes brush against his fingertips. Butterfly kisses, that's what my father called it. Alexei leans in, taking my chin in his fingers and turning me to face him again as he kisses me on the lips. There is none of the fierce desperation he showed me last night. Only softness and sweetness.

"You don't scare me one bit," I tell him.

A flicker of something akin to worry crosses his

face. "Perhaps you should be a little afraid of me, Daisy," he says solemnly.

I can't help but laugh. I know he's right. I'm sleeping with a killer, someone who has actually murdered in my name. I can't explain my feelings. Not towards him, not towards what he did. But I don't feel any bit afraid of him.

"You've saved my life, Alexei. You've taken care of me. You've showed me nothing but kindness. Do I have any reason to fear you?"

He stares at me for a few moments in silence, clearly contemplating my words.

"I would never intentionally hurt you," he says finally.

"Exactly," I say with a groggy smile, as if he made my point for me.

He stands up, taking my hand and giving it a little tug. "Come on."

I tilt my head to one side. "Where are we going?"

"The forest," he says cryptically.

I stand up beside him, squinting in confusion. "For what? Why?"

He raised an eyebrow, looking amused. "You want to learn how to shoot, yes?"

I grin, my heart leaping in my chest. "Right now?"

Alexei nods. "Early morning in the woods is the perfect time and place. Come with me."

The two of us dress slowly and methodically, easing into the morning. To my relief, Alexei lets me borrow an almost comically oversized shirt that hangs like a short dress on me. The hem barely skims the middle of my thighs, but it's better than wearing the same old dress and slip again. I slide on my ballet flats and scoop my hair back into a flouncy but tidy ponytail.

Alexei puts on his usual daily uniform of jeans, boots, and a white shirt.

It's kind of funny how between the two of us, he looks pretty put-together, while I look rather like a little girl wearing her father's t-shirt. But it doesn't matter. I find that I don't feel as insecure and hyper-critical of myself when I'm with Alexei.

He has seen me without makeup, my hair unwashed, my clothes slept-in and bedraggled, and he finds me sexy and desirable just as I am. That's a new revelation to me, and one that makes me rethink my perspective on how I present myself to the world. With Alexei behind me, I could hardly bring myself to care what most other people think about me. He's all the assurance I need, all the backup I could ask for.

With him, I feel free.

Once we're dressed, I make us a couple of sand-wiches and pack them into a little bag I find in the kitchen. Then, with Alexei leading the way, we march out of the house into the summer morning.

I take deep breaths as we walk, drinking in the light breeze, the smell of flowers and pine on the air, the hazy light casting the world in pastel colors. As we make our way to the forest, we stop at a little wooden shed with a locked door. Alexei takes out a key from his pocket and unlocks it, reaching inside to retrieve a large rifle. My eyes widen at the sight of it. It's even bigger than the antique gun I keep at my house. I wonder if I can even hold it well enough to aim it.

Alexei gives me a silent, reassuring nod, and I set my worries aside for the moment. We keep moving, crunching over sticks and twigs, listening to the bright, cheerful singing of little birds in the trees around us. There's dew on the grass and leaves, and I can feel the soft, wet earth muddying up my shoes, but I don't care. I grew up running around these woods, forever frustrating my daddy who just wanted me to keep my clothes clean for at least long enough for him to catch up on laundry. But as a child, I was borderless, unstoppable. Nothing about the forest frightened me— not the birds of prey swooping through the trees, the dizzying labyrinth of paths that could confuse even the most seasoned hikers and explorers, not even the hulking bears and wolves stalking through the underbrush. I feared no poisonous plants, no buzzing insect or spinning spider. I was happy in the woods.

Today, I feel that old happiness rising up in my heart once again. This is where I belong, where I feel free and at home.

"I love these woods," I muse aloud, smiling up into the green leafy canopy.

"It's very peaceful," Alexei agrees.

"Nothing like this in the Big Apple," I comment.

He shakes his head and chuckles. "No. Definitely not."

"Did you live in New York City all your life before you came here or did you ever get to go hiking around the forest as a kid?" I ask curiously.

There's a long pause, the silence punctured by our footsteps crunching over the leaves, the breeze through the branches, and the ever-present bird songs. Then he answers, "I spent my youth doing a different kind of exploring."

"In the city?" I press him, suddenly deeply interested in the answer.

"Yes. You might be surprised at how much exploration there is to be had in the mean streets of the big city," Alexei remarks.

I pick up the pace, jogging to catch up to him. Looking up at Alexei with a big, dopey smile, I push him for more. "Like what? How?"

He glances down at me with his brow furrowed, but a smirk on his lips. "You ask a lot of questions, Daisy."

I shrug. "I'm a curious person. Besides, it seems only natural to want to know more about the man I've been shacking up with for the past couple of days. We may have skipped a few of the usual steps in regards to a first date, but that won't stop me from playing twenty-questions with you to catch up on it."

He seems to chew on the question for a moment as we trek deeper and deeper into the forest, the rifle still propped against his broad shoulder. Then he says, "I did not have very much guidance as a young boy. Not a lot of boundaries to keep me close."

"You mean you were like a latchkey kid?" I suggest.

"Yes. I suppose you could call it that," he agrees a little hesitantly. "My guardians were... rather far removed from my upbringing. I was provided for in all the usual required ways: food, shelter, clothing. Nothing elaborate, but they kept me alive."

"That doesn't sound like a particularly nurturing environment," I say sadly.

He gives a solemn, slow shake of his head. "No."

"Who were they? The people who raised you, I mean," I ask.

"What?" he retorts, frowning.

My face flushes and I hurry to explain myself, hoping I haven't stepped over the line with my questioning. "You said 'guardians' rather than parents, so I just assumed..."

"Oh," he interrupts placidly. "Yes. My parents were not involved. I was raised by someone else. In New York."

"What about your parents, then?" I pipe up. It hits me a half-second later that I might actually be treading into touchy territory. I have lots of great memories of my childhood, of being raised by my father, despite the fact that somewhere deep in my heart, I did always long for a mother figure in my life. But I know that not everyone was so lucky as I was.

"Sorry if that's too personal for me to ask," I add hastily. "I'm just wondering."

"It's alright," he says in a soft voice.

"I forget that some people might not have the same happy feelings about their parents that I do. I apologize," I tell him.

He reaches over to put a hand on my shoulder, giving it a gentle pat. "Don't be sorry. I don't mind the questions. I'm just not fully accustomed to having to think about these things. Not for a very long time, at least."

"Did you ever know your parents?" I ask cautiously.

"Yes. Well, not that I can remember now," he says. I tilt my head to the side, confused.

"I'm sorry, I'm not sure what you mean," I reply with a shrug.

Alexei heaves a sigh, looking up into the canopy of vibrant green above us. Then he slowly answers, "They sent me away when I was very young."

"Sent you away? But why? I don't understand," I

counter. "You mean like they put you up for adoption or something?"

"Not quite. It was more... specific. More intentional than the situation you are probably envisioning right now," he says.

"Specific? How?" I press him. Lord, getting him to give me the full story is like pulling teeth. I know I should probably back off and let him remain swathed in mystery like he seems to prefer, but I just can't stop. For some reason, it's like the more he withholds from me, the harder I want to push to get to the bottom of it all.

"My parents lived in a very poor, very isolated village in *Sibir*," he says, the name rolling off his tongue in a surprisingly thick accent. It's jarring to hear, because normally his accent is fairly faint. Of course, his manner of speech still singles him out somewhat from the crowd here. His accent certainly could never be mistaken for a Midwestern country drawl.

"Siberia?" I verify, wide-eyed with awe. He nods.

"Yes. They were very old when they had me. My mother had assumed her childbearing days were long past, and yet, there I was," he says. His tone is both sad and slightly amused. He goes on. "They knew there was no future for me there in the village, and they were afraid that there would be no one to look after me when they passed. So, they sought out a way to get me out of the country, send me someplace better. They found what they were looking for when a man from Moscow came traveling through. When I was a few years old, they entrusted me to him and he promised to take me away to America."

My jaw drops. "They just... handed you off to some stranger?"

Alexei smiles wryly. "Desperate times—"

"Desperate measures," I finish the sentence, shaking my head in disbelief. "Well, what happened after that?"

He stops and looks around, holding out his arm to stop me, too. "What is it?" I ask, worried that perhaps he has heard someone approaching.

"This is a good place to practice shooting," he decides, taking the rifle in his hands.

"Oh," I reply, remembering why we've trekked all the way out here in the first place.

"To answer your question," Alexei begins as he takes a cartridge of bullets out of his back pocket and starts loading up the gun. "That man did, in fact, take me to America."

"To New York City?" I ask.

He nods. "Yes. Just as my parents asked him to."

"So, did that man raise you? Was he your guardian?" I question.

Alexei snorts and shakes his head. "No. Not at all. He dropped me with this older woman by the name of Rada. She ran an unofficial home for young boys in the Bronx."

"Like a foster home?"

"One might call it that, I suppose. She provided food, clothes, a place to sleep. It was crowded. I had many brothers. We slept four to a room."

"Oh wow," I say, letting out a low whistle. "I'm suddenly glad I was an only child."

Alexei gives me a soft smile. "Compared to what my childhood would have been like in Siberia, it was fine. I grew up surrounded by friends who came from similar backgrounds. I spent my days roaming the streets with my band of brothers, exploring abandoned buildings, scavenging for items to sell. The city was our forest."

"Well, that doesn't sound so bad," I remark, although deep down it still sounds rather terrifying and bleak to me.

"You don't have to lie, Daisy," he says, unaffected. I blush again. He takes a pair of foam ear plugs out of his pocket and hands them to me. I look at him blankly for a moment and he nods, gesturing to his ears. I hurriedly squish the plugs into my ears as instructed.

He pulls me to him, my back against his chest, and he lowers the rifle into my hands, crouching down slightly to balance it on my shoulder. His breath tickles my ear when he says, "I learned much of what I needed to know about the world from my older brothers. Rada fed and clothed me, but it was my brothers who raised me. Taught me how to be a man."

Placing his hands over mine on the trigger, he cocks the gun. I swallow hard, my heart already pounding.

"What happened to them?" I ask meekly, my voice barely above a whisper. I can't even hear my own voice through the ear plugs, and Alexei's words are muffled when he speaks.

"They were recruited. And it was only natural for me to follow," he says simply.

With Alexei guiding my hands and fingers, he points the gun at a thick, knobby oak about twenty yards away. We fire the gun and I let out a yelp of surprise as the recoil snaps me back against Alexei, who somehow seems to have kept his stance perfectly. Even with the plugs in my ears, the resounding bang of the gunfire sends my ears ringing. My chest is heaving, my jaw dropped, and my eyes round as saucers. And yet, even with the fear coursing through my veins, the adrenaline fills me with a feeling almost like euphoria.

We spend the next few hours or so going over the ins and outs of gun ownership and use, Alexei showing me how it all works, the mechanics of the gun itself, how to aim, how best to position it to reduce recoil. My ears are ringing and my heart racing, but even I have to admit it feels kind of good.

I didn't grow up with guns, even though most

ALEXIS ABBOTT

our friends and neighbors hunted and went shooting for leisure. It simply was not part of my life, personally. Apparently, my mother despised guns, and as a result, Daddy maintained a mostly gun-free household even after her death. Well, with the exception of the antique gun I still have for show.

When we're finished, I feel much more comfortable with the weapon than before, and much more knowledgeable about Alexei's background, where he comes from, who he is.

He never ceases to somehow enthrall me and comfort me at the same time. I don't know how he does it, but I hope he never stops. We find a relatively clean clearing to sit down in and eat our sandwiches, just chatting breezily and enjoying the beautiful surroundings. It just feels right, somehow, despite the undeniable strangeness of the moment. I can't believe I'm out here in the woods with a real, genuine murderer.

I look at him in the soft dappled sunlight, the faint wind ruffling his hair, and it's hard for me to reconcile the two sides of him I know exist. He's a dangerous man. A true bad boy. I thought Dean was bad, but Alexei makes him look like tame by comparison.

Then I think about what Alexei had told me, about Dean torturing animals. About him being sadistic and enjoying the pain of a living creature. The way Alexei talked about it, I could hear his

I HIRED A HITMAN

disgust. Alexei might be a killer, but he still has a compass. A moral code.

Dean was the truly dangerous one.

And now he isn't a problem anymore, not for me, not for anyone. All thanks to Alexei.

I smile at the thought, relief warming my heart as I look at him. I feel so safe with him, and it's exhilarating. Like the two of us are invincible together, especially now that I know how to fire a gun if I have to.

I feel empowered.

Alexei and I walk back to the farmhouse afterward, hand in hand, crunching through the picturesque woods in comfortable silence. When we get back inside, he asks me if I would like to go home or stay longer.

"I want to stay as long as you'll let me," I tell him honestly. "But I do need to retrieve my truck from the Sugar Creek Tavern. I can't keep letting it sit there in the way."

Alexei smiles. "I'll take you there. We can pick up something for dinner while we're out. Perhaps a change of clothes for you, too."

"Oh, yes," I laugh. "That would be nice."

The two of us pile into Alexei's truck and take off toward the outskirts of town, listening to the classic rock station on the radio.

I feel free. Happy. Completely at ease for once in my life, despite everything that has happened. I reach across the console to take Alexei's hand, and he gives it a gentle squeeze. It feels like all is right in the world.

We pull into the parking lot behind the Tavern, and to my relief, my old truck is still sitting exactly where I left it a few nights ago. But when we pull up to the other side of it, my heart skips a beat and my blood runs cold.

"Alexei… do you see that?" I breathe, raising a shaky hand to point at a word spray-painted in blood-red on the driver's side door. I turn back to look at him and see a grave, solemn scowl on his handsome face.

"Shit," he grunts.

ALEXEI

"*S*inner?" Daisy says, reading out the word written on her truck in big, sloppy red letters that run in trails of paint. She looks up to me with large, hurt eyes. "Who in the hell would...?"

My jaw is clenched, and my eyes are locked on the truck in front of me. My mind is racing with the implications of what I'm looking at, and none of them are good.

"What does it mean?" she asks. "I don't know anyone who would do something like this. Unless..."

"Unless someone knows what happened to Dean," I rumble in a low tone, and her head snaps back over to me with eyes wider than I've ever seen them.

"Oh my god, what? How could they? Oh my god oh my god, what if-"

"The body is hidden," I say, "but there's *always* a

185

chance it could be discovered. And if not, one of his friends or family might have seen us leave together that night at the bar. If that happened, there's every chance one of them suspects us."

Her face goes pale, and I put a hand on her shoulder and look at her seriously. "These are all just possibilities—we don't know yet."

Daisy takes a deep breath in and nods.

"If someone saw us leave together, maybe it's just someone... mad at me for going home with a man. Or even drinking late at night in a bar," she muses, clearly more to calm her own nerves. I regret even offering up my alternative.

"What we do know is that regardless, we need to act fast."

"What do you mean?"

"We need to leave," I say in a low, ominous tone.

"We can't just leave the truck here!" Daisy says, looking alarmed.

"Would you prefer driving that thing around town in the condition it's in?" I ask, gesturing to the thing. "It'll draw attention that we can't afford to have right now."

"If we leave it here, people are guaranteed to start asking questions," she fires back. "This isn't New York, remember? This is a small town in the country. Everyone knows everyone, and everyone knows damn well that's my truck. If we just leave it for everyone to see, then people are going to start asking questions and go looking for me to ask about all this. And that's going to lead someone to us, especially if..." She swallows hard, shaking her head. "If someone suspects me as being part of a murder."

I clench my jaw and look at the truck again, but I know she's right. My mind is still reeling with different possibilities for what might have triggered this.

"Fine," I say. "Get in the truck and drive it close behind me. Don't stop for anything."

"Where are we going to go?" she asks, heading toward the truck, a slight spring in her step. If I didn't know better, I'd think the excitement was starting to get to her in a good way. Am I worried I'd corrupt her, taking her virginity. But not like this.

"I have to check on something," I say. "And while we're at it, we have to get that truck hidden."

"Hidden? Where?" she asks, suddenly defensive.

"Nowhere that it will come to harm," I assure her. "Just trust me, Daisy. We have to move quickly here. Wait!" I shout, and she freezes in her tracks with the door of her car open.

I hurry over to the front and crouch down, getting on my back and sliding my way under the front of the car. I check over the machinery with a furrowed brow, making sure everything is normal before pushing my way back out.

"What the hell was that about?" she asks.

My mind races to find a way not to tell her that I was checking for a car bomb.

"Just making sure that whoever vandalized the car didn't mess with any of the interior, either," I give as a half-truth, but the look on Daisy's face after I say it tells me she's smart enough to guess at the implications of my words. She doesn't press me for more, so at least she trusts my judgment.

I look up at the darkening sky, the last glimmers of sunlight disappearing over the horizon. "Darkness will serve us well for what we're about to do," I say.

"You know there's a way to say that that doesn't make you sound like a vampire, right?"

In the middle of a tense situation, Daisy brings a laughing smile to my lips.

"Just stay close," I say, and she rolls her eyes and gets into her truck.

A moment later, we pull off into the darkness, and our headlights are the only things around for a long ways, the only spots of light in the inky blackness of the country roads.

My hands are tight on the wheel, and I keep checking my rear-view mirror to make sure that Daisy is still behind me.

I don't even have time to think. Right now, all I need to do is move, and quickly. I have to get Daisy out of harm's way first and foremost. Just being in a separate vehicle makes me nervous in that regard. I find myself glancing in the mirrors to look even

I HIRED A HITMAN

further back from her truck, almost waiting for someone to show up to give us trouble.

I hope Daisy is right. I hope it's nothing more than some hoodlums trying to slutshame her.

But one thing remains the same, though. I have killed, and while I don't want to do so again, I will, if it means keeping Daisy safe.

Before long, we pull up to one of the many dirt roads leading into the woods, and I lead Daisy about half a mile down the trails, finally coming to some low brush that I've noted the past few times I've driven by the area. I come to a slow stop, and I get out of the truck expecting to have to take over for Daisy, but she catches my lead and carefully drives her truck into the brush.

I help her out and get some more coverage on the truck. Neither of us say a word as we work, as if our voices would attract any more attention than the drive out here took.

When it's done, I get back into my truck, and Daisy gets in the passenger's side, giving one last look at her vandalized truck before I pull away.

"Is he far from here?" Daisy asks quietly.

"What?"

"Dean," she says, looking over at me as I turn us around and start heading in the opposite direction. "I'm guessing you didn't just leave him wherever you did it. If we have to lie about what happened, we should have our story straight, right? Isn't that how this works?"

I take a deep breath and grip the wheel tightly as I drive. She isn't entirely wrong, but I can sense the meaning behind her words. I need to smooth her feelings over before I can have her total cooperation. And frankly, she's entitled to that—Daisy has played along with more over the past few days than most people would even think of.

Part of me thinks she's just attracted to the danger, to the risk and excitement she thinks my life has. I don't want to hope for anything better than that. Not now.

"I staged it perfectly," I say at last. "There should be no way that this can come back to us, but I don't have eyes everywhere. I met him in his kitchen, and I shot him while he was diving for his shotgun. I took him and the gun to the woods after cleaning the house. I thought there would be a witness when someone stopped outside the house, but it was only the mailman—I watched him from the window in the shadows. He made his delivery and left, never suspected a thing."

"Did you take the body near here?" she asks, suddenly panicked.

"Of course not," I say. "I wouldn't lead you to stash your truck near the body, that would be foolish."

"Right, right," she says. "Sorry, I just…"

I HIRED A HITMAN

"No, you're right to ask those questions," I say. "Never assume your partner is competent. That's the whole reason I work alone so often."

I give her a moment of silence to reply, but when she doesn't, I go on.

"I took him to the woods behind his house, down a trail he seems to have used himself often. I set up the body and shot him in the head with his own weapon where my bullet entered. It did enough damage that it covered the wound I gave him. I'll spare you the details, but I removed my bullet as well. It's as close to perfect as it can get to looking like a hunting accident—as if he dropped his shotgun and hit him in the head. There are some forensic scientists who might be able to find the difference in the bullet wounds in his head during an autopsy, but those scientists are not anywhere near Broken Pine, Nebraska."

I glance over to see how Daisy is taking the explanation. She looks shaken, but she keeps her eyes forward. I move a hand over to her knee and give her leg a gentle squeeze. She puts her hand over mine instead of pulling away, and I feel its warmth spreading through my arm. It soothes my own pounding heart.

"You're doing well," I tell her quietly.

"I wish I didn't have to," she says.

"Me too," I say. "Just remember—"

"He deserved it," she says, and there's resolution

in her voice. The surprise and shock has faded, and she's seeing the truth in my actions. Maybe it isn't just an attraction to excitement, then. "I'm with you there, I think. I'm just worried about what it means for us."

"It means," I say, "that I'm going to take measures to keep you safe."

She looks at me with a furrowed brow. "And what does *that* mean, exactly?"

"It isn't safe for you to go home, for starters," I say. "You will be safer with me than you would be alone. I suggest you call in sick as soon as possible. You're going to stay with me for a while until I can get some eyes on the outside and figure out what's really going on."

"With you?" she says, sounding concerned. "Alexei, I want to be with you, don't get me wrong, but...are *you* safe?"

"I'll worry about me," I say. "I dealt with one hick, I can deal with more if I need to. But not until they come to me. If we're apart, then it will just be easier for them to come after you and keep me distracted at the same time, if that truly is what's going on here."

"If?" she asks, sounding even more concerned. "I thought we were both on the same page here?"

I frown. "Yes. But I like to keep all possibilities open so that I can never be surprised by the truth."

"And what possibility are you thinking about, exactly?"

My frown stays in place as I come out of the woods and start blazing down toward my house. "Nothing I want you to worry about unless you have to. You have enough on your mind as it is."

Soon, we arrive at my home and pull into the driveway. I get out first, checking around the yard before getting Daisy from the car and leading her by the hand to the door. Once we're inside, I lock it behind us.

I turn around and see Daisy standing there before I have a chance to turn the light on, and I realize she looks terrified. My looming form in the shadows has just dragged her across the town to help cover up a murder she might be suspected of being involved with, and I've just locked her in with me.

There isn't much distinguishing her from a hostage.

I take a deep breath and set my hands on her shoulders, squeezing them, and she steps forward to accept a large, tight hug.

"I'm scared, Alexei," she says. "I just need to get that out for a second."

"That's okay," I say, rubbing her back and feeling the warmth of her small frame pressed against me. "You're allowed to be afraid. I have you."

"I'm glad," she says, and I feel my heart warm a

bit. I'm more afraid for her than I am for myself. For so long, I've worked alone, doing what I needed to in order to survive. I never had to worry about anyone but myself. It was easier that way.

But much lonelier.

I put one of my hands on her head and kiss the top of it before rubbing her gently.

"It's okay to be afraid—what we can't afford is to let the fear cripple us. Let it drive you, let it make you do things you never thought you could do, take risks that were beyond your imagination, but you must not let it paralyze you."

"As long as you're here, that won't happen," Daisy says.

I look down at her and meet her gaze. "I need to show you something now," I say. "Follow me."

I make my way down the hallway, toward the fake closet at the far end of it.

"This place isn't just my home," I say. "I have it well stocked for emergencies, in case anything happens."

"Were you expecting something like *this* to happen?" she asks.

"Not specifically," I say, "but in my line of work, you never stop being cautious unless you are prepared to meet a violent death."

I open the panel that reveals the secret chamber I have hidden behind the back of the fake closet, and as the door slides open, I hear Daisy gasp behind me, putting her hands to her mouth.

"Alexei…"

I step into my chamber, then turn to look at her, surrounded by racks upon racks of guns and supplies.

"His friends might be cocky, but I'd like to see them take on this."

She steps inside, looking around like she's in a museum of the most delicate artifacts in the world, which is about the level of caution I would hope from the first stranger I've ever let into this sanctuary.

"How long have you had this?" she breathes.

"I had contractors who didn't ask questions," I say simply, "and I made some modifications after the fact. The original was a little less conspicuous."

"Christ," she murmurs, looking at one of the sniper rifles I have mounted on the wall. "Are you planning to assault the damn town?"

"That's not the part we're here for," I say, and I make my way to a large set of drawers at the far end of the room. I open the middle shelf, and with the sounds of rattling plastic and paper, its contents slide around roughly. Daisy appears at my side, and she looks down at the contents with an open mouth.

Inside are passports, false identification papers from a dozen different countries bearing my face, travel and work visas, two laptops, and a dozen burner phones.

"Is this...?"

"All forgeries, all highly incriminating," I say curtly. "If we want to be prepared, then we have to be ready at the drop of a hat to run. Are you prepared to do that?"

"Wait, what?" she says, suddenly looking panicked. "Run? Alexei, I... my whole life is here. This whole town practically raised me. I can't just drop all that and leave."

"I've been in homes I haven't wanted to leave either. But circumstances might not give you a choice. If Dean's friends and family decide that you're trouble, do you really want to stick around and find out what they plan on doing?"

She frowns, but she seems to see the logic in what I'm saying.

While she thinks on that, a flashing light catches my eye. I turn and look at one of the burner phones, and my eyes lock onto the dull blue flash of a text alert.

At that moment, it hits me—I usually keep an eye on these phones, in case I get a word from some of my trusted contacts back east. I've simply been... distracted from my diligent watch lately.

I pick up the phone and check the message on it.

What I read makes my face go pale as a ghost.

They found you. Run.

The date on the message...is three days ago.

I feel like the world around me has frozen in time and is starting to fall apart. Never, *never* have I been so careless as to let something like this go unchecked for this long.

I'm a fool for thinking I could ever live a normal life with a beautiful woman and a half dozen kids running around our feet. That's the life for different men.

I took every precaution, measured every single step to ensure that nothing would go wrong at any point. I had my methods down to an art. But I took one wrong move. I fell for Daisy, and it made me careless.

"Fuck!" I say, suddenly and loudly, and I pace back and forth in the room, staring at the message before I break the phone in two in my hands.

"What? What is it?!" Daisy shouts back, looking panicked.

"I never should have let this happen," I growl, storming back over to her.

"Alexei-"

"I never should have let *you* happen," I say.

My old life has found me.

They want blood.

And now, it's too late to run.

"*A*lexei, slow down!" I yell at him as he paces back and forth. "What is going on? You have to fill me in."

He glances over at me, his eyes steely and cold.

"I should never have let you get so close to me," he growls.

My stomach twists into knots as a shiver runs down my spine.

Across the room, my phone beeps. I ignore it.

"W-What?" I ask, taking a step forward and shaking my head in confusion. I flash back to that first fateful evening at the Tavern, when a tall, mysterious stranger sidled up next to me at the bar counter and paid for my drink. "What do you mean? 'Let me get close?' You're the one who came after *me*, Alexei. Don't get it twisted."

I can see a muscle in his jaw tightening and

twitching, his hands curling into tight fists. His chest rises and falls with a heavy sigh and he looks away. "And I can see now that was a mistake."

Tears spring to my eyes, but I'm not just hurt. I'm angry. Again, my phone beeps.

"Where the hell is this coming from?" I demand to know. "We were in this together *five minutes ago* and now suddenly you're looking at me like I'm some huge liability."

He gives me a pained expression.

"Daisy, you're not the liability. I am," he says quietly.

"What do you mean? You're the one who saved my life! You saved me from Dean Ashcroft. You took me from that bar. You kept me protected. You kept me safe. You taught me how to shoot a gun. I-I'm prepared for anything now," I protest.

He pinches the bridge of his nose, shaking his head.

"But you shouldn't have to be prepared for anything. It's not your life. It's not your way."

"You're not making any sense, Alexei," I tell him. I walk over to him and take his hand away from his face, holding it with both of mine. I gaze up at him even though he won't meet my eyes. "You're the hero of this story. We're in this together," I assure him.

"I am no hero. I have done terrible things," he replies softly.

"You were following orders," I remind him.

"I have the blood of many, many men on my hands," he adds.

I lift his hand to my lips and gently kiss his palm, then press it against my cheek, leaning into the warmth as I look up at him with fierce adoration.

"Bad men. You told me they were all bad men. Like Dean. Men who deserved exactly what they got," I affirm.

He looks at me, finally, and I feel almost dizzy with the radiance of his gaze. There is intense sadness in his eyes, his jaw still tightening as though he's desperately trying to hold something back, but I don't know what it is. I am almost afraid to ask.

My phone beeps again and I groan in frustration, rolling my eyes. "God, this is not the time for this," I mutter. I let go of Alexei's hand and cross the room to snatch up my phone just outside the closet angrily. I slide open the screen, taking note of how dangerously low the battery is. I'm amazed it has any juice left by now, actually. But it has just enough for me to open up my social media app and check the many notifications lighting up in bright red. As I do so, my eyes widen and my heart starts racing.

"Alexei," I gasp. My hands start to shake.

"What is it?" he asks, worried about me. He rushes over, staring at me.

I hold up my phone, pointing to the many, many messages posted on my account. Messages from some local guys I only know tangentially, who are a few years older than me. Messages from friends of Dean's. Angry, accusing messages.

SLUT.

How dare you cheat on Dean?

JEZEBEL.

I know what you did!

SKANK.

Everyone thinks you're such a good girl, but I know the truth!

BITCH.

You're gonna pay for what you did to him!

"Who the hell are these people?" Alexei growls, taking the phone from me and scrolling through them with a scowl on his face.

"I guess someone at the Tavern must have seen me go home with you that night. Or maybe Dean told his buddies what he saw before he... before you..." I trail off, going pale.

"Before I killed him," Alexei finishes flatly.

"Yeah," I murmur.

"Do you know any of these men very well?" he asks, handing the phone back to me.

I shake my head.

"No. Not at all. Dean was pretty secretive about his personal life, at least with me. I mean, I guess he told all these guys that he was seeing me, but that's no surprise. It's a small town, and Dean was even more well-known than I am. Of course people would believe him that we were going out. But you know what this means, right?" I ask, brightening up.

Alexei is silent, looking concerned and contemplative.

"It means that whoever spray-painted my car is just some dumb local. Some idiot who was just seeking out some petty revenge because I supposedly cheated on his buddy. That's good news, right? It is!" I insist, laying my hand on Alexei's powerful arm. He looks at me sharply and shakes his head.

"It doesn't matter," he says.

I furrow my brow, looking at him like he must be insane.

"What do you mean? Of course it matters! This means we're off the hook, Alexei! It means that nobody suspects that you or I had anything to do with Dean's death. They're just mad at me for 'cheating' on him! It's a dumb redneck prank, not some elaborate conspiracy," I explain, a chuckle of relief coming out.

But he doesn't look convinced or relieved at all.

I glance over at the stash bag full of extra passports, weapons, and burner phones. I point to it and say, "We don't have to go on the run or whatever, we're fine. We can stay here. Nobody knows the full story about what happened. Hell, nobody even knows Dean isn't still alive, right? Maybe it'll blow over. Maybe everyone will just think he ran off to join the rodeo or something. He was just crazy enough to do something stupid like that, anyway, and everybody knew it. There is no reason for anyone to suspect us. Sure, it's a hassle and a pain in the ass that these stupid guys graffitied my truck, but who cares? In the long run, that doesn't matter. Everything is going to be okay."

"I wish it was as simple as you think it is," he sighs. "I wish I could live in that world."

I take a half-step back, blinking in confusion at his words. I cross my arms over my chest and glare at him, feeling offended. "Excuse me? Are you calling me stupid?" I ask.

Alexei rushes to reassure me.

"No, of course not. I'm calling you *innocent*."

"Why does everyone keep calling me that? I'm not innocent, Alexei! I'm involved with a murder cover-up, okay? I went home with a dangerous man from a bar, a dangerous man who saved my ass and killed the man who was stalking me. And you know what? I'm not upset that the asshole is dead. I don't care. No— I'm actually fine with it. I'm happy about it. Maybe someday that will come back to bite me in the ass, but right now? I'm just relieved it's not worse than I thought. This is a problem we can deal with. We can handle this. And whether you like it or not, I am a part of this story now. I'm partly to blame, and I'm in this with you. Right beside you. For better or for worse," I declare firmly.

But he's in his own head, impervious to my

words. "I should never have allowed this to reach you. I screwed up," he mutters to himself.

"What's wrong? Why aren't you as happy about this as I am?" I demand, throwing up my arms and waving them to get his attention. I even stomp my foot, feeling rather like a petulant child, but unable to hold back my confusion and anger any longer.

"Because," he says calmly, "you are not the only one to have received a message."

"What did it say?" I ask him, raising an eyebrow. I had momentarily forgotten about him breaking one of the phones in my excitement.

He straightens up, looking more imposing and stoic than ever before. I could almost be afraid of him if I didn't know how much goodness is in his heart. I can feel the light radiating from him. I know that underneath the scars and the tattoo and the darkness that has descended around him like smog, Alexei is a good man. And I will stand by him until the end, no matter what happens, no matter what he's about to tell me.

"I should have kept this to myself. I should have stayed solitary," he growls.

"But you didn't," I reply simply. "And now I'm here. And I'm asking you to let me in. To show me the truth. I don't care how ugly it is. I don't care how much danger it may put me in. I need to know the truth, Alexei. You're not going anywhere without me. You can't get rid of me that easily."

He nods, realizing how serious I am. He opens his mouth to speak.

"In New York, I was on trial," he says.

"I know," I answer.

"For murder," he says.

"I know."

He pauses, fixing me with an intense stare. "It was not my first, and as you know, it was not my last. But it was the first and only time I have been in court for my crimes. I intend to never do that again."

"But you got off," I remind him. "You got out of there scot-free."

"Not quite," Alexei replies darkly. "I was scarred. I was tired. I wanted out of the game. I could have gone to jail for killing a man who deserved to die. I was acting on my orders, just as I always did. I was a weapon for the Bratva, nothing more. I was untouchable, living outside the restrictive bound-aries of the law. I applied myself to a different moral code, one that is incongruent with the law of the land. And I had accepted my fate, my place in the world. I was not pleased with it, exactly, but I had long since made my peace with my sins. But being in that courtroom— it changed something inside of me."

"How?" I ask.

"I decided to live my life for myself, to stop following orders. I had been an obedient, valuable member of the Brotherhood for years. Even before I had officially been recruited to join their ranks, I was being groomed for that life. Rada, my rather neglectful foster mother, was taking money from the mafia. It was not Rada who paid for my clothes, my meals, my bed. She was merely a tool of the Bratva, keeping tabs on the young boys who would be funneled directly into the fold once we were old enough," he explains.

"You wanted to be free," I breathe.

Alexei nods firmly. "Yes. I wanted to live free. And not just in regards to prison. I escaped that dark fate by the skin of my teeth. The witnesses were cowed into withdrawing testimony. Without them, the case was purely circumstantial. The Bratva moves in shadows. They leave no trace, no trail. I was no different. I am very well-trained, Daisy, and I left not a hair nor print for the law to follow. I have always been good at cleaning up my own messes," he says with a wry smile.

He pauses to gather his thoughts and I wait patiently.

"After I walked out of that courtroom, surprised to find myself a free man once more, I decided I was finished following orders that could put me in prison. I had been a somewhat willing captive of the Bratva since the very first moment my feet touched American soil. From time to time, it had felt good, even safe, to belong to something larger and more powerful than myself. But after the trial, I was done.

I went to the Brotherhood and I asked them for their blessing to depart, to start over somewhere far away, far from the mean streets of the big city. Far from the accusations and the bloodshed and the commands that ruled my life. I needed to be my own man."

"And they let you leave?" I ask, totally taken aback.

"Yes," he says. "But only because I had served them so dutifully. Even when I was in police custody in the months leading up to the trial, I never let slip a single word to incriminate any of my brothers. I insisted that I acted alone, of my own accord. I kept my lips shut tight, refusing to allow the Bratva's name to come up. The police suspected they were involved. Some of them knew without a doubt that I was acting on someone else's orders. But I refused to give in to their questions. I stayed quiet, even to my own detriment. I was lucky to walk out of that courtroom a free man, and because I had performed so well under pressure and remained utterly loyal to my brothers, the Bratva decided to reward me with that most elusive and unimaginable of gifts: the freedom to walk away from it all."

"And so you came here, to Broken Pine," I murmur.

He nods, walking over to put his hands on my shoulders, peering down at me.

"Yes. I came here because I thought it would be

quiet. A place to hide, to live simply and without adornment. No one here would question me, and my past would stay behind me in New York. And for some time, it worked. I was right. Broken Pine was quiet and unassuming, the perfect place for a dangerous man to hide. After all, what better place for a wolf to hide from his pack than in the midst of the flock?" he says, smiling wistfully. "But then, something changed."

"Me," I sigh.

"Yes, you. Daisy, from the moment I laid eyes on you, I knew it would be impossible for me to stay away. And when I saw that dark shadow, that prick, hovering around you, I could not let him keep you. I took him down, and I don't regret my decision for a moment," Alexei admits. "I only regret that my decision has drawn undue attention to me, and by extension, to you."

"But the graffiti… what does that have to do with you?" I ask plaintively. "It's just some dumb prank. It has to do with *my* crime, *my* sin, not yours."

"You're right. It has nothing to do with me except that it widens the target to include you along with me," he answers.

"The target?" I repeat. "But if we're the target, who's pointing the gun? I don't understand, Alexei. You're not suggesting that some local idiot from this podunk town has some crazy mafia connections or something, right?"

"Of course not," he says.

"Then who the hell is after us?" I ask.

"Someone from my past. Someone who must have a grudge against me. I assume it is one of my former brothers, someone convinced that I did not keep tight-lipped while under police custody. Someone who wants revenge. Or silence. You see, Daisy, the Bratva is like a powerful ship sailing the seas. And if there is one tiny hole in the body, that can spring a leak and take down the entire ship. I assume that whoever is after me right now considers me that leak," Alexei tells me. "And he plans to plug the hole, by whatever means necessary."

"Oh my goodness," I mumble, wide-eyed with fear.

"Goodness has nothing to do with it," he replies gruffly.

"What are we gonna do?" I question, grabbing his hand. He lifts it to his lips and gives my fingers a gentle kiss, sending a shiver down my spine.

"I was planning to leave," he tells me flat-out.

"Without me?" I ask, feeling my heart breaking.

Alexei pulls me into his arms and hugs me close, kissing the top of my head. "Only to give you a chance at surviving. But I can see now that there is no way to cleanly remove you from the target. We're in the crosshairs together, and now I must think of somewhere we can go, somewhere we can hide. The message I received came days ago."

"Days ago?" I repeat, pushing back to look up at him in horror.

He nods. "Unfortunately, yes. I will admit that my time here in Broken Pine has made me complacent. I stopped checking my burner phones on a constant basis like I used to. I had started to believe I truly could escape my past. It felt safe here. And the last few days has been a whirlwind. I neglected my duty to my safety. But I was wrong to be so foolish. My sins back in the city are far too great to have expected them to stay in the past where they belonged. But we can't stay here, Daisy. We need to move."

"Where?" I ask, terrified.

"I don't know," he sighs. "Not here. Not your house. We need someplace with a strategic vantage point. Somewhere from which we can watch the town closely."

Suddenly, an idea occurs to me and I gasp aloud. Alexei looks down at me, worried.

"What is it?" he asks.

"I know where we can go."

ALEXEI

$\mathcal{M}$y motorcycle roars down the road toward the outskirts of town, and I feel truly free, despite the fact that I should be feeling anything but that right now.

Daisy's arms are around my waist, holding onto me from behind and peering over my shoulder as I blaze down the road. Wind whips around us, and I feel her body heat warming me from behind. It feels *right* in a way I can't explain.

If only we weren't fighting for our lives.

It's too warm for my leather jacket, but I'm wearing it to conceal the two pistols I have strapped to my sides. There's a hunting knife strapped to my belt, and a pair of sunglasses shield my eyes from the glaring light above.

There's a small pack of equipment stored in the motorcycle, including a couple of bedrolls and enough rations to last us a while. The truck was too dangerous to take into town, I decided. If someone has been after me for at least three days, they'll have seen my truck, but I haven't ridden my bike in over a week, so whoever is after me isn't going to be expecting that.

And if I know the people who are after me, they have certainly been watching me.

I don't even know how many are out there. It could be one, or it could be a dozen.

I slow the bike down as we get close to the old mechanic shop that Daisy had told me about. It's a run-down looking place, but it looks like it has stood for many decades. There's an antique feeling to it, and the *For Sale* sign hanging on the front makes it look vaguely haunted in an eerie sort of way.

Behind the shop is the beginning of a corn field that stretches far enough that I can't see the other side. Nebraska corn fields rise up like the tides of an ocean, far and wide and sometimes endless. I've gotten used to them since settling in Broken Pine, but they can still be disorienting if you stare into them for too long.

As we slow down, the engine gets quiet enough that I can listen to the stillness of the town, and there's a strange energy around the auto shop. It's as if time slowed down here, or simply stopped.

I pull up to the shop, and Daisy hops off with her ring of keys jingling in her hands as she moves to one of the padlocked shutter doors. A moment later, she pushes the door up, and it starts sliding on its own. She slips inside and stops the mechanism just as it's far up enough to let me inside with the bike.

I pull in, and indeed, it looks like nothing inside has been updated since the 80s. Light filters in from the windows far up above, but it's deathly quiet in here.

She closes the door behind me, and I kill the engine and swing my leg over the bike, parking it.

"Well," she says, putting her hands on her hips and looking around. "This is it."

"It's a fine place," I say, taking my sunglasses off and tucking them into my jacket. "Your father should have been proud of it."

"You don't have to lie, but he was," she says, laughing softly. "Sometimes I wish I'd been able to take after him and keep this place going, but you know how life goes."

"That I do," I say. "Do you know somewhere comfortable we can get settled in here before we start looking around old memories?"

"Good thinking," Daisy says. "Let me go check out the office, make sure it's not infested with hornets or anything."

I chuckle as she heads toward a small office space at the back of the shop, just next to the rear exit. I furrow my brow as I notice the door is open—wide open, in fact. Daisy doesn't pay it much mind, so I assume people around town are just honest enough that it's never been something to worry about.

Then a noise at the opposite end of the shop snaps my attention away.

I look over to a stack of old crates full of auto parts, and I see a fallen, rusty muffler moving ever so slightly on the ground, as if something recently bumped into it and it hasn't stopped spinning on its side.

My instincts kick in, and my whole body tenses.

If I were an assassin hunting a man in a small town, where would be the ideal place to hide out?

An abandoned mechanic shop.

I silently take one of my guns out, and I start making my way toward the crates, aiming it at roughly man-height where the muffler was.

I'm ready to shoot at any moment, finger on the trigger. I can't let him know I'm coming for him, or it could endanger both me and Daisy. I pray a silent prayer that Daisy stays busy with the office for a few more moments.

If I'm careful, I can at least get the drop on the man behind the crates.

Once I'm close enough, I take a silent, deep breath, then round the corner with my pistol aimed.

...and I hear a scream.

I aimed my pistol about where a man's head would be, planning to hold him at gunpoint. My barrel is about two heads *above* the face of the source of the noise—a boy of no more than nine years old, who falls on his rear and scrambles back with wide eyes at the sight of me.

"I'm sorry!" he splutters, face absolutely terrified. "I'm sorry! I'm sor-!"

He starts to repeat the same line over and over again, but I kneel down and lower my weapon, putting one hand on his shoulder and a finger to my lips.

"Shhh, shhh, it's okay," I say in the most soothing tone I can manage. "You're not in trouble."

"Promise?" he asks.

"Yes," I say. "But I need you to tell me what you're doing here. Who are you?"

The boy has mousy hair and a thin face—he isn't treated well, clearly, and he looks nervous at my question. "Dad told me not to talk to strangers," he says.

"Is your Dad nearby?" I ask softly.

Another pause, and this time, he wrings his hands. "Promise you won't tell."

I put a finger to my lips again and nod.

"I ran from him," he says. "This place looked really cool, so I came here to hide."

"Why are you hiding from him?" I ask, my tone as gentle as I can make it.

"He's mean," the boy says, and I feel anger rising in me. "He got meaner since we moved here. He yells at me to be quiet and not talk to people, so I came here instead."

I open my mouth to say more, but something clicks in my mind. "...when did you move here?"

"Three days ago," he says.

Three days.

What are the odds...?

I stand up and hold out a hand. "Stay here," I say hurriedly, and I jog to the office to find Daisy. I need to get her and see if she can help me get information out of this kid for all our safety's sake before we get him the help he needs.

But when I look into the office door, it's empty.

My heart misses a beat.

She's gone.

DAISY

"Help! Oh god, help me! Alexei!" I cry out, my heart thumping so hard and fast that it's difficult to breathe evenly. My lungs are on fire, my throat tight and constricting with fear. It's like the adrenaline pumping through my veins is paralyzing me rather than giving me added strength. There are a pair of rough, big hands grasping my upper arms in a vice grip, yanking me along and dragging me over the sharp gravel rocks toward the corn field that presses into the back border of the old garage lot.

There was a time when this place was a happy one, filled with light, fond memories that I would revisit on my down days. I have strolled by the garage a thousand times, just reminiscing about how lively and cheerful the place was back when my father was still alive to run the business.

ALEXIS ABBOTT

There always used to be loud classic rock music bumping from the stereo system, the twang of dueling guitars, the pebbly roughness of rock 'n' roll singers projecting nearly a half mile down the street in either direction. My father ran a tight ship, and he personally trained every one of his employees, making sure everyone was equally competent in every area of the job. I used to love watching him work while I sat there swinging my legs, singing along with the music in my childlike soprano.

But even as a little girl I was afraid of the corn field behind the garage.

Something about it has always frightened me. Something about the vast expanse of green and gold waving lazily in the breeze, the dense stalks and peeling husks riddled with tiny squirming insects while mice and snakes scampered around on the ground.

My childhood fear is now coming to fruition.

I am being dragged, kicking and screaming, into the maze.

"Help me, please!" I shriek, reaching up with trembling hands to claw at my captor's grip. But he is silent and efficient, yanking me closer to clap a hand over my mouth. He quickly muffles my desperate cries, and before I can try and vise his hands away from my lips, he uses his other hand to grab both of my wrists and pin them together with what feels like a zip tie.

Moments later, he crouches and holds my head between his knees tightly, whipping out a filthy red paisley bandana that smells like stale cigarette smoke and sweat. To my horror and disgust, he ties the bandana securely around my head, stuffing the musty fabric into my teeth to staunch my attempts at screaming for help. Within a few terrible minutes, my mouth is gagged and my hands are bound, and suddenly I am a thousand times more helpless than I was before.

I start whimpering in terror, kicking and wriggling to get away from him with every little ounce of strength and determination I have left. But this hardly helps. In fact, all it does is make my captor angrier.

He yanks me to the ground and gives me a swift kick to the ribs, effectively knocking all the oxygen out of my lungs. I cough and splutter for air, hyperventilating through my nose as the bandana makes it nearly impossible to breathe through my mouth. The pain is intense, radiating from my ribs up and down over my entire body.

Tears burn angrily in my eyes as I instinctively pull my knees up closer to my chest, curled in the fetal position on the filthy ground. My eyes roll to the side, wide and round with fear as I look up at the man hovering over me with a hateful scowl. I can hardly make out any of his features, though, because of the aggressively bright sunshine. It's noon, and the bright light through the corn stalks turns every-thing a hazy citrus-greenish color. Between the fear, pain, and lack of air to my lungs, my vision starts to swim and my head pounds mercilessly.

I shut my eyes and cough, shivering even as my body sweats in the summer heat.

"Quiet," the man hisses. He reaches down to pull me back up into a sitting position, then hoists me up over his shoulder. My face is slumped down over his back and every step he takes causes me immense pain from jostling the undoubtedly bruised area where he kicked me.

I can't see much, and my mind is flooded with panic and agony. It's too full. Too frantic to form any coherent, helpful thoughts. All I can breathe in is the smell of cheap body spray mingling with musky sweat. Everything is pain and dread as the mystery man carries me away, deeper and deeper into the labyrinth of tall stalks, farther away from the only man with any chance of saving my life—again.

I don't know why this is happening. I don't understand. It all happened so quickly, and I'm still struggling to catch up and get my brain up to speed. I was in the garage, walking out the back to look around for danger while Alexei spoke to... spoke to someone. And then suddenly, the danger I was looking for found me instead.

But why me? Who could possibly be after me?

I'm *nobody.*

The man repositions me, hoisting me more securely over his shoulder and I groan with another rush of incredible pain. I close my eyes, feeling weak and sick to my stomach, angry at how easily I can be captured, how easy a target I am.

In the crosshairs together.

That's what Alexei said.

I should have known to be more careful. Being with Alexei has made me too cocky, too brazen, too sure of myself and my place in the world. But how was I supposed to know that something like this would happen right now? Now, in the bright, cheery light of day.

My mind, confused and overwhelmed, retreats into the dark but comforting crevasse of my old memories. Of being a little girl, only six or seven, and lying in my bed.

I was staring up at the ceiling, my heart pounding and my eyes burning with tears. My night light on the wall had burned out, the little bulb needed replacing. And I was suddenly plunged into the kind of all-encompassing natural darkness one can only experience out in the country, away from the ever-present glow of the city lights. The room was pitch-black and I was terrified, whimpering and crying in my bed.

A moment later, there a knock at my bedroom door and I yelped in terror. My father came rushing in, pushing the door open to allow a thin pillar of light filter in from the hallway. He knelt at the side of my bed and asked if I was okay.

"Did you have a nightmare, sweetheart? Are you okay?" he asked me, truly concerned.

Tears were streaming hot down my cheeks. I shook my head.

"I'm afraid of the dark," I told him.

I can still see in my mind's eye the slow spread of his smile across his softening features. Pity and love reflected back in his gaze. He kissed me on the forehead and told me, "That's perfectly normal, Daisy. Everyone is a little bit afraid of the dark. But here's what you're going to do: the next time you're in the dark and you're scared, I want you to close your eyes and picture the sun. Imagine you're outside running around in the bright light. Pretend it's daytime and you're happy and safe. Nothing bad ever happens in the daytime, right?"

I remember nodding.

His logic was sound, at least to my childish ears.

"Okay, Daddy."

He tucked me back in and said, "I love you." Then he left.

I closed my eyes and I did what he told me to do. I smiled to myself in my little bed, imagining that the warm glow of the sun was on my skin, and suddenly, I was no longer afraid of the dark.

Nothing bad ever happens in the daytime, right?

I jolt back to the present moment, suddenly choked up and more fearful than ever. *Daddy, you lied*, I think to myself. Sometimes bad things do happen under the happy light of the sun.

But I can't just give in. I have to fight.

I summon what little power I can manage, channeling my fear into anger. I somehow swing my legs, bending them to knee him in the ribcage, almost in the exact same spot where he kicked me earlier. He groans in pain and shock and immediately drops me. I fall to the ground with a horrible thump, agony shooting through my prone body. I nearly bite through the bandana as I squeal in discomfort. But as the man reaches to grab me again, I pull my legs back and then jab them forward, kicking him squarely in the ankles with both feet. He crumples to the ground, momentarily disabled.

This is your one shot, the voice in the back of my head tells me.

Run.

With my heart racing so quickly I can hardly remember to breathe, I scramble to my feet and take off through the green stalks, my hands still bound and my mouth stuffed with the bandana. I can feel the sharp leaves and ticklish corn silk brushing against me as I run. I don't have a single clue which direction I should go. I'm too short to see over the heads of the stalks, and the blinding noon sun makes me disoriented. It doesn't matter. I know if I only keep running I will find the edge of the field eventually. And besides, I can't turn back and risk being caught by my captor again.

I don't even dare look behind me.

I just run.

ALEXEI

My heart is pounding, and the adrenaline coursing through my veins keeps me from even feeling the green stalks my sprinting body is pushing aside.

I have a knife in one hand, gripped tight and ready to fight. A gun won't be of much use in these fields, but I have mine still loaded and at the ready at my side.

I never should have taken my eyes off Daisy, even for a second. But I had no idea we had ended up right on top of our pursuers. It all clicked in my head the moment I realized Daisy had been taken.

Whoever is after me came here dragging along his unfortunate son, who ran away from him at the first chance. He then went looking for his boy, tracking him to the auto shop right around the same time that we showed up there.

Bastard probably heard us pull up and hid.

And he's good at leading me on a winding chase through the cornfield.

I swear, the stalks distort sound in here. My hearing is excellent, and I've been tracking them as well as I can, but Daisy's captor is moving fast and strategically. This is no amateur. I catch his trail one moment, but when I think I'm closing in on him, he changes his direction, and I hear him behind me. The three of us would look like damned fools from a bird's eye view.

But when I hear him cry out, my heart leaps, because I know Daisy has hurt the son of a bitch.

That's my girl.

But I also know that her action has put her in danger. This man isn't after Daisy, not in the long term. He's after me, and if Daisy is an expendable way to get to me, then he doesn't have any reservations about killing her.

At the same time I hear the cry, I hear sudden, hurried footsteps running—these ones are faster than the man's, and I know it has to be Daisy running as fast as she can.

For a split second, I have a choice.

I can try to follow the kidnapper and try to take him down, or I can head for Daisy directly in hopes of cutting him off.

It's a decision I make in no time.

Changing my course, I race after Daisy's footsteps.

After barely ten seconds of sprinting full-tilt, I see the edge of the cornfield, and I realize why the chase through the rows was so chaotic—he was taking us on a loop, winding us in circles the whole time.

Bursting out of the field, I see Daisy still running away from it, and she looks over her shoulder at the sound of my exit.

Immediately, she comes to a stop, running back in my direction.

I catch her as she jumps into my arms, and I hug her for half a second before I take the gag out of her mouth and use the knife to cut her free.

"Oh my god, Alexei!" she gasps.

"We're not out of the woods yet," I say, cutting her off. "Where is he?"

"I don't know, I left him behind when—"

She gets cut off again, but this time, it's by the sound of an engine roaring toward us. On instinct, I grab Daisy and pull her to the side just a moment before a truck comes barreling out of the cornfield, headed straight for us.

I feel the bumper brush against my back, barely missing us as I hit the ground with Daisy cradled in my arms.

When I look up, I recognize the truck, and all my questions are answered.

"Move!" I shout to Daisy, and I stand up to run with her, back toward the auto shop.

The truck doesn't follow us, though. It speeds off down the road, barreling toward the countryside.

He's trying to get away.

We dash back into the auto shop, where I catch the little boy crouching by the shutter door I came in through.

"I wasn't doing anything!" he squeaks as soon as I rush inside with Daisy.

"Who is he?!" Daisy asks.

"Later," I tell her, then look to the boy. "Open the doors!"

He scurries to the mechanism he watched Daisy use earlier, and he hits the button just as I jump onto the motorcycle, and Daisy gets on beside me. I rev the engine, and I roar past the boy's wide-eyed face, blazing down the road to follow the man who tried to hurt the person I love.

Love.

That's a word that's going to take some getting used to.

I see the truck of the kidnapper up ahead, and I know I'm going to be gaining ground on him fast. My motorcycle can blaze faster than a truck can, no matter how much ground he has on me. The only question is how well armed he came.

"Who is that?" Daisy shouts at me as I lean

forward, reaching for my gun to make sure it's still there and ready for use.

"Demyan. An old 'friend' of mine," I shout back. "A rival. Real bastard. He took the jobs I turned down—killed innocents."

"And now they're sending him after you?"

"No," I say, "This is a personal grudge. He wants to kill me of his own accord to get favor with the bosses. That's why he brought his kid along—he doesn't want anyone to know what he's doing."

I'm sure every other word is getting lost to the wind as I shout it all back to Daisy, but it doesn't matter. The only thing that matters is that I put him down.

I gain ground on the truck, and when I'm close enough, I pull my pistol out and aim for a tire. I fire, but it pings off the back of the bumper and ricochets off into the fields. I have to be careful, or an innocent farmer could get hurt.

But I have to end this soon, or police will get involved.

I see the driver fumbling with something, and the next moment, a pistol appears in the window. He blind-fires at me, but I've already veered right and aimed another shot at his truck.

I slow down as I do, trying to steady my aim, but this time, Demyan catches on and pulls a smart move.

He accelerates, then uses the handbrake to swing

his truck around, forming a barrier for me to hurdle toward.

If I can't react in less than half a second, Daisy and I are about to get flattened against the side of the truck.

I veer left, so sharp that I feel the balance of the bike going out from under me as it lets out a squealing screech of rubber against asphalt. I see the whites of Demyan's eyes as he levels his pistol at me.

It feels like time is thick and sluggish all around me. I hear Daisy screaming as she hugs me tight, her face in my back. My shooting arm is extended. I bring the sights up, and for the slightest fractions of a second, I can see those whites of Demyan's eyes through them.

I fire.

My bike skids off the road and into the dirt of the ditch. With the sudden drop, I turn the bike into the fall and keep it from laying down. It's disorienting, and I can feel my vision spinning, but I can see the truck clearly.

There's no cover out here, no place for a tight and dramatic shootout, just me and Daisy and a motorcycle.

I level my pistol and aim at the truck again as my vision steadies itself.

Nothing happens.

"Are...we still alive?" Daisy asks.

Without responding, I get off the bike and

approach the truck with my gun still out. I don't see Demyan in the vehicle. I make my way to the door and pull it open, gun aimed at the driver's seat.

Demyan's body falls from it, a single bullet hole in his head where my shot landed true.

EPILOGUE

"*Y*ou may now kiss the bride!"

The cheers of the crowd ring out so loudly that they nearly drown out the dulcet tones of the small string band. I grin up into Alexei's handsome face, feeling so overcome with joy. He whispers, "I love you, Daisy. From now until the end of time." Only I can hear him, but that's just fine. Those words are meant only for me.

He cups my face in both hands before slowly leaning down to press his lips against mine in a soft, adoring kiss. I lean into his warm touch, trembling with awe and happiness. I never imagined this could be my reality.

As he kisses me, the crowd cheers louder and louder, and I laugh against his lips when I hear the specific hoots and hollers of Harriet and Jolene in the front pew.

"That's my girl!" Jolene cries out proudly.

When we finally break away from the kiss, Alexei takes my hand in his larger one and we turn to rush down the narrow aisle between the pews dragged into neat angling lines. We could have gotten married in the chapel, but as it turns out, the little church isn't actually big enough to hold all our guests— because in a town like Broken Pine, a wedding is regarded as a town-wide affair. An excuse for every inhabitant of our sweet little country town to dress up, put on their nicest cologne or perfume, and pile into whatever building is big enough to accommodate us all.

Being that this is a country wedding, and that Alexei and I are both passionate about horseback riding, it only makes sense that our ceremony is being held on his sprawling farmland property. The biggest building on the acreage is this one: the gigantic barn with its vaulted ceilings and unmistakable, centuries-old wooden beams. Even though we obviously worked hard to clean it up and make it spotless, there still remains just a subtle hint of the scent of hay and gunpowder. It doesn't bother us, though. It just gives the whole event a more authentic barn-wedding feel to it. A bespoke country ceremony, the two of us surrounded by the people who adore us, by those who have known me and known my family line for decades and decades. And now none of them can look at me with pity

236

anymore. I'm not just the lonely, overworked daughter of Jacob Jenson these days— I'm the smiling, laughing, glowing new wife of the most handsome and charming man in town.

Through me, the townspeople have learned to adore Alexei. They see how well he treats me. How he protects and cares for me. They know he's the reason why I smile. And he's also the reason for my natural glow... because even though we haven't told everybody just yet, I'm pregnant. I'm just now beginning to show, and I chose a wedding dress appropriately— an empire-waist gown that cleverly disguises the start of a noticeable baby bump. The doctor has assured us that we will be having a boy, and we already plan to name him after my father.

The ceremony fades into the reception, the band striking up the country music while we eat amazing food cooked with love by Harriet and her crew from Maud's Diner. Barbecue, fried chicken, macaroni and cheese, green bean casserole— and of course, an elegantly rustic wedding cake big enough to feed an entire town of hungry folks. Of course we don't all fit neatly inside the barn, so the reception spills out onto the bright green fields, with long wooden tables of charmingly mismatched lengths and shapes. We eat happily, my guests laughing and talking and making toasts with their champagne flutes while Alexei and I sit at our own table, lost in love and over the moon.

After the meal, the sun is beginning to set as the music swells louder and couples take to the makeshift dance floor. Alexei leads me to the center of the floor, the two of us spinning and twirling joyfully together.

I have never known happiness like this. The threat against our lives is over. The man who attacked me, who tried to take Alexei down, was just a rogue agent of the mafia out for revenge. His mission was not sanctioned by the Bratva, and so they viewed his defeat as a triumph. Plus, Alexei promised me that they're giving Demyan's son a better life, without constant fear.

And Dean, well... It turns out more people than I thought knew he wasn't all that he seemed. The entire town seemed to let out a collective sigh at his tragic, accidental passing, and more than a few people whispered to me that they were happy I found a *good man*.

With the continued blessing and protection of the Brotherhood, and the love and embrace of the townspeople here, our life together is off to one hell of a beautiful start.

As the moon rises to hang over the dance floor like a luminous white lantern, I lean into Alexei's arms and kiss him.

"I love you, Alexei. More than anything in this world," I whisper to him.

"I never knew quite exactly what I was searching

for when I came all the way out here," he says softly, "but now I know. Every misstep, every bend in the road, every so-called mistake— it has all led me to you. We were meant for each other, Daisy, and I will cherish you until the end of my days."

I used to live day by day, afraid to think about the future. But not anymore. Now, I am excited to see what the future holds. Every single day brings more joy, and I can't wait to spend the rest of my life this way.

THANK you so much for reading! I hope you enjoyed <3 If you have a moment, please leave a review. Other readers are dying to know what you thought.

I have plenty more bad boy romance for you, so make sure you check out my other books on the next couple of pages, and sign up for my newsletter to be notified when I have a new release on the way!

~Alexis Abbott

ALSO BY ALEXIS ABBOTT

Romantic Suspense:

HITMEN SERIES:

Owned by the Hitman

Sold to the Hitman

Saved by the Hitman

Captive of the Hitman

Stolen from the Hitman

Hostage of the Hitman

Taken by the Hitman

The Hitman's Masquerade (Short Story)

THE KILLER TRILOGY:

Book 1: Killer for Hire

Book 2: Killer Desire

Book 3: Killer on Fire

SEXY SEALS

Sweetheart for the SEAL

Sights on the SEAL

HOSTAGES:

Stealing Her

The Assassin's Heart

Killing For Her

Abducted

STEPBROTHERS:

Ruthless

Criminal

STANDALONES:

Betting on Love

Hunter's Baby

I Hired A Hitman

Vegas Boss

Rock Hard Bodyguard

Innocence For Sale: Jane

Redeeming Viktor

Romance:

Falling for her Boss (Novella)

Most Wanted: Lilly (Novella)

Bound as the World Burns (SFF)

Erotic Thriller:

THE DANGEROUS MEN SERIES:

The Narrow Path

Strayed from the Path

Path to Ruin

ABOUT THE AUTHOR

 Alexis Abbott is a Wall Street Journal & USA Today bestselling author who writes about bad boys protecting their girls! Pick up her books today if you can't resist a bad boy who is a good man, and find yourself transported with super steamy sex, gritty suspense, and lots of romance.

She lives in beautiful St. John's, NL, Canada with her amazing husband.

facebook.com/abbottauthor

twitter.com/abbottauthor

instagram.com/alexisabbottauthor

bookbub.com/authors/alexis-abbott

pinterest.com/badboyromance

youtube.com/AlexisAbbott

CONNECT WITH ALEXIS

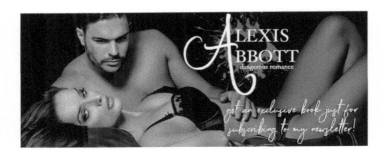

Get an EXCLUSIVE book, **FREE** just as a thank you for signing up for my newsletter! Plus you'll never miss a new release, cover reveal, or promotion!

http://alexisabbott.com/newsletter

ACKNOWLEDGMENTS

Thank you to my amazing Patrons. I'm constantly humbled and grateful for your support.

Ramona Cabrera
Melissa Hedrick
Virginia Swanson
Dawn Daughenbaugh
Don Doss
Stacie Currie

If you'd like to join them — and get my ebooks or paperbacks — you can find me here on Patreon.
https://www.patreon.com/alexisabbott